D0946217

LEOMAN

MARK R. MURRY

Archway Publishing books may be ordered through booksellers or by contacting:

Archway Publishing
1663 Liberty Drive
Bloomington, IN 47403
www.archwaypublishing.com
844-669-3957

ISBN: 978-1-6657-0182-2 (sc)
ISBN: 978-1-6657-0183-9 (e)

Library of Congress Control Number: 2021901117

Print information available on the last page.

Archway Publishing rev. date: 02/02/2021

This book is dedicated to my beloved wife, Dorothy, who has always encouraged me to follow my dreams; my beautiful daughter, Annabelle, for giving me a reason to keep writing; and to my family, friends, and other loved ones, who continue to inspire me.

CONTENTS

PROLOGUE: WHO IS THE BOY IN WHITE?

How did all of this happen? Why did all of this happen? These were the questions I thought as I woke up and realized where I was. I was in my car. The windshield, for some reason, had been shattered. Why was the windshield busted? Why was the front of my car bent up like a crumpled piece of paper? Why was there a fallen lamppost laying on top of the front hood? I climbed out of my car. Then I started to panic. Somehow, I had crashed my car into a light post. I looked around, thinking of how my parents were going to kill me when they found out Annie and I had.

Annie!

That's when I saw that she was in the passenger seat, bleeding. I ran over to her door and pulled out her limp body, praying to God she wasn't dead.

Not again … Please, God, not again.

"Annie! Annie! Please don't be dead! Please, Annie, wake up!" I shouted.

"Mmmm … Leon?" she finally groaned, waking up.

I sighed with relief. "Oh, thank you, Lord. Thank you."

"What happened?"

"It's okay, you're going to be okay," I tried to reassure her.

Her eyes then widened with fear as she quickly sat up.

"What happened?" She panicked as she quickly sat up. "Where's that little boy that you swerved around?"

"What little boy?"

Then realized what she meant. I remembered a little boy standing in the road and jerking the steering wheel to avoid hitting him.

"Oh man, where is he?"

That's when we started looking around for him, calling out to see where he was and if he was okay.

"Yes?" said a little voice that made us spin around.

It was him. Thankfully, he looked like he was okay. He was a little ten-year-old boy with blond hair and blue eyes. He was wearing a white T-shirt, khaki shorts, and white tennis shoes. Despite everything that had just happened, he had a calm, almost curious look on his face.

"Hey, are you okay?" I asked as Annie checked him for injuries.

"What's your name?" Annie asked.

"I don't know, ma'am," he replied.

"Where are your parents?" I asked.

"I don't know, sir," he replied.

"What were you doing in the middle of the street?" Annie asked.

"I don't know, ma'am," he replied.

"Not much of a talker, this one," I remarked sarcastically.

"Cut it out, Leon," Annie replied sternly. "We have to get him to a hospital."

"How are we supposed to do that?" I asked. "The car's totaled."

"We need Leoman," she replied.

"No," I said sternly.

"Leon, there's no other way," she said.

"Forget it, Annie!" I exclaimed angrily. "Leoman is dead."

Then I called for an ambulance, and we both sat down on the sidewalk near the wreckage that used to be my car. After a while, I could hear the sirens of the approaching ambulance coming down the street while Annie and I waited by the car. When it came to a screeching stop, the EMTs jumped out of it and started checking us for injuries.

"Are you hurt, young man?" asked one of them.

"I'm fine, ma'am," I replied. "Just a few scrapes and bruises."

"What's your name?" she asked.

"Leon Garrett."

"How about you, young lady?" asked her partner.

"Annie Jones," Annie said.

"Are you hurt, Annie?" he asked.

"I'm fine, sir," she replied. "Where's the little boy?"

"Okay, Leon, Annie," the first EMT said. "We're going to take you both to the hospital to get checked out."

"What about the little boy?" I asked.

"What little boy?" the second EMT asked.

"The little boy in white who's standing right there," I said.

Then I realized that he had managed to run away while the EMTs were busy with us. Although this wasn't the first time someone had managed to get away from me.

An hour had passed as we waited in the emergency room while the doctors checked us for injuries. Annie and I hardly said a word to each other. Probably because she was still mad at me for the situation that I had gotten us into.

"Annie," I finally said, "I am so sorry—for everything I've put you through."

"It's okay, Leon. But I just don't want to talk about it right now."

I decided to turn my head away and keep my mouth shut, for the sake of our friendship and because of how much I still cared about her deep down in my heart.

Annie's parents came in with concerned yet sad looks on their faces.

"Excuse me, Doctor," said Mr. Jones. "We'd like to speak with our daughter in private."

"Of course, Mr. Jones," the doctor replied. "We're almost done with her examination."

"We need to speak with her now, Doctor," Mrs. Jones said. "It's urgent."

"Well, all right. You may speak with her, but please do it out in the hallway."

"Thank you, Doctor," Mr. Jones said. "We won't be long."

Even though they shut the door to the examination room, I could hear them despite my hearing not being as great as it once was.

"*What*?" Annie screamed. "What do you mean I'm adopted?"

"Please, Annie, just calm down and let us explain," Mrs. Jones pleaded.

"No! What I want to know is why you would keep this a secret from me?"

"Because your medical records are under a different name—your birth name," Mr. Jones replied, trying to calm her down.

That's when they started arguing all at once. I stopped trying to listen because I couldn't understand what they were saying. But even now, I must wonder myself. Why did Annie's parents keep her adoption a secret from her? Did they know something about her parents? Who could they have been? I would eventually be finding myself asking these questions and more.

Then I saw two strangers wearing masks approaching Annie and her parents. They pulled out their guns as I heard Annie's parents shout for help and saw the strangers trying to kidnap Annie.

"Let go of me! Mom! Dad! *Help*!" she screamed.

I got up from my bed and ran out into the hallway to confront one of the kidnappers.

"Get your hands off her, scumbag!" I shouted.

As I prepared to throw a punch, of the kidnappers hit me in the face, breaking my nose.

"Nice try, you little punk!" He chuckled.

"Ooowwww! Ooohhhh!" I groaned.

I felt so dazed that I almost passed out right then and there. As I regained my focus, the gunmen grabbed Annie and started running away.

"Annie? Annie!" I shouted.

I tried to catch up to them only to get shot three times in the chest when one of the kidnappers turned around and pulled the trigger. At first, it felt like a sudden shock. Then it started to burn with unbelievable pain. As I dropped to my knees and then fell face down, I found myself reaching out to Annie as the kidnappers escaped with her.

"No … Annie …" I groaned.

Normally, I would've been able to heal within a few minutes, get back up onto my feet, track them down, and save Annie. Well, Leoman would've been able to. Now I was just a poor deluded fool bleeding to death on a hospital floor, all because I thought I could make a difference as a superhero. But for you to completely understand how I got to this point, I need to take you back a couple of months ago, to when my best friend and I were standing on a street corner next to a hot dog stand, eating lunch as he talked about another urban legend that I secretly used be in another town—in another lifetime.

CHAPTER 1
WHAT IS THE NEXT ASSIGNMENT?

Who or what is Leoman? That would be me, Leon Garrett, sixteen-year-old intern photographer for the *Sedalia Star.* At least, that's what I was a few weeks ago before all this happened. I live in Sedalia City, in the Midwestern state of Indiana. However, I used to live in Salemburg, a small town near the Missouri River. We moved here about a year ago after my dad got transferred to the Sedalia City Police Department to take over as the Chief of Police. That's how it all started.

There we were, standing by a hot dog stand on a street corner, eating lunch, while Joe was talking about an urban myth he had become obsessed with called the Beast of Salemburg, who had been terrorizing local criminals. I was wearing my red-and-black hoodie, blue jeans, and white tennis shoes, with my press badge hanging around my neck so I wouldn't forget it.

"Well, maybe it's because you lived in a town that's about as famous as Transylvania is for Dracula," said Joe.

Joe Vantrice is my best friend and internship partner. He is about six feet tall, with a pale complexion, black hair, and light-blue eyes. He was wearing a green shirt, black jacket, blue jeans, and black tennis shoes. He had been my best friend ever since I moved to Sedalia City. The people who live here used to call this town heaven on earth. What a big fat lie that is these days.

"Are you talking about that silly urban legend again?" I laughed. "You know there's no such thing as a monster where I come from, right?"

"Hey, man. The Beast of Salemburg is no myth. He's real. Heck, he's the reason that criminals are terrified to come out at night."

"Look, Joe. If the Beast were real, how come the *Salemburg Journal* stopped printing his sightings and exploits?"

"See, that's the weird thing. About four years ago, he disappeared."

"Just like that, huh?" I looked at him sarcastically.

As we started walking down the street, we passed the local newsstand.

"Cool!" I exclaimed. "The new issue of *Red Lion Ride*r is out! Awesome! This is the one where he finally fights the Mad Mastermind!"

"Leon, I love you like a brother," Joe began, "but don't you think that you're a little too old to be reading that book?"

"Says the guy who believes in the Beast of Salemburg. Besides, you know it's my favorite!"

"I know, Leon." He rolled his eyes. "Believe me, I know."

I looked at my cell phone and noticed what time it was.

"Hey, Joe. We'd better get to the *Sedalia Star*, or Mr. Jacobs's going to make our jobs disappear."

We walked over to Joe's hippie van, as I called it, a green 1969 Volkswagen van.

"Peace and power for the hippie van, brother," I laughed.

"Hey, man, at least this baby gets us from point A to point B."

I hated to admit it, but even though it was an old, out-of-style piece of junk, it did get us to different places when it was needed the most. Joe's the same way as a friend. Cool and calm, with a very clever sense of humor and a heck of a lot of patience with me. He's also a great partner when it comes to our job. The *Sedalia Star* is one of the local newspapers in Sedalia City. Joe and I work there as a reporter and a photographer with our school's internship program. Joe is the investigative reporter, and I work alongside him as his photographer. My high-functioning autism really helps my eye for detail, which, in turn, helps me with my pictures. Speaking of my autism, the story of how Joe and I became close friends is kind of a funny story.

It was a few months after we met. We had some of the same classes together. We were walking down the street from the bus stop to our neighborhood when the city's emergency sirens went off. It was only a test, but the sound was so loud it felt as if my eardrums were going to explode. While trying to get away from the sound, I accidently ended up inside a beauty shop. After the sirens stopped, I realized where I was and ran out embarrassed. Joe was standing just outside the door and stopped me.

"Are you okay, Leon?" he asked as we walked back to my house.

"Yeah, I'll be fine."

"Do you want to tell me about what happened back there?"

That's when I finally told him I was a high-functioning autistic person, that my social skills were not the best unless I took my daily medicine to help stabilize my mood and with my concentration. To my surprise, he was very cool and accepting about it. He didn't laugh at me or abandon me on spot as if I were some monstrous freak, like a lot of people I used to know, and he's been in my inner circle of friends ever since.

A little later, after I was done reminiscing, we got in the door of the *Sedalia Star*, and we heard a big, loud, and familiar voice.

"Garrett, Vantrice, my office now!" bellowed Mr. Jacobs.

"Yes, sir!" I called out as we hurried into his office.

Mr. Jacobs has a ridiculously small, dark office; the only light in the room comes from two pairs of LED lights on the ceiling and his computer screen. The reason the room is so dark is because he always keeps the blinds on the windows nearly shut. The windows take up about half the wall, nearly touching the ceiling. They extend from the edge of the doorway to the back wall where his cheap metal desk sits. There are two tall, thin wooden bookshelves on both sides of his desk and two sets of filing cabinets on both sides of the doorway. Usually, there are two chairs at the front corners of his desk, but this time, there were four, two on the front-left corner and two on the front-right corner.

The two chairs on the right, I assumed, were meant for Joe and me. Because sitting in the chairs on the left were two girls who Joe jokingly called our competition.

Mr. Jacobs was a man in his late forties to early fifties, with a pale complication and a tall, thin build. He was wearing a white button-up dress shirt, black dress pants, and black dress shoes.

"What's going on, boss?" Joe laughed. "Are you pulling the second-stringers from getting your coffee?"

"Excuse me!" Annie retorted. "But if anyone's the second-stringer around here, it's you, Joe!"

"Hey, guys. Come on," I said calmly. "Remember that we're all still friends here."

"Yeah," Annie said as she held out her hand for a handshake. "So may the best pair of interns get the front page."

I blushed for a split second because she was holding her hand out to me. But then I snapped out of it and shook her soft, gentle hand.

Annie Jones and Rachel Peters are two more of my closest friends. Annie is a skinny, tanned girl with dark-brown eyes and long dark-brown hair, tied in a ponytail. She was wearing a teal T-shirt, blue jean shorts, brown sandals, and brown-rimmed glasses. Rachel is a little taller than Annie, with light peach skin, blue eyes, and short blonde hair. She was wearing a pink blouse, blue jeans, and pink flip-flops, which matched her cheerful and bubbly personality.

"Sit down, boys," Mr. Jacobs said.

Joe and I did as we were told and sat down.

"So what's up, boss?" asked Joe.

"Okay, everyone, listen up and listen well!" began Mr. Jacobs.

"I'm only going to say this one time. I'm giving the four of you to an opportunity to get a story featured on the front page. The pair of interns that does the best job on their next assignment will get the front page and a two-hundred-dollar bonus. Got it?"

"Yes, sir!" all four of us said in unison.

"Good," said Mr. Jacobs. "Now, here are your next assignments: Garrett and Vantrice, you two cover the press conference of the recent murder of Byron 'Big Daddy' Jackson. Jones and Peters, you two cover the Martin Baker interview."

We all sat there waiting for Mr. Jacobs to go on, but he didn't.

"What are you waiting for? Time is of the essence; I want this done today. Not tomorrow, not next week—today!"

As we were heading out of Mr. Jacobs's office, Joe stopped me just before I reached the doorway.

"Wait for me outside the door, okay?" he asked.

"Sure pal, but why?" I asked.

"Just wait for me. I'll be out in a few minutes."

So I did, and he shut the door right behind me.

After ten minutes of waiting, I heard the loud voice of Mr. Jacobs. Even though the closed door muffled it, I could still hear him loud and clear through the door yelling at Joe.

"How many times have I told you? We don't print fiction; we print facts!" bellowed Mr. Jacobs. "Now, stop wasting my time with your urban legend garbage and get on that story!"

Then Joe opened the door and came out of the office.

"I'm on it, boss." Joe sighed. "Come on, Leon, let's go to the chemical plant."

We reached the chemical plant twenty minutes before the press conference started.

"All right. Let's split up. You go get pictures of the crime scene while I talk to the cops," said Joe.

"Okay, see you at the conference," I said.

When I got to the crime scene, I took out my camera and started taking pictures of the broken window, which was covered by a tarp.

Then I went down to the street and took pictures of the marked-off street, where the victim's body hit the ground. While I was doing so, I overheard a few police officers describing the incident as they watched the city morgue's van drive away.

"Yeah, apparently the victim just walked out the top floor window of his skyscraper office and plummeted all the way down to the street," said one of them.

"No kidding?" said another one. "Hey, did you see that strange symbol craved into his head?"

"Yeah, that weird backward Z?" said the first one. "Why?"

"The coroner said it looked like he carved it into his forehead," the second one said. "They found him clutching it in his left hand."

After I got over my initial squeamishness, I took all the pictures I needed and went over to meet Joe at the press conference.

When I got to the press conference, it had already started. I went up to Joe, who was just finishing interviewing the last police officer on the scene. I showed him the pictures I took and told him about everything I had seen and heard at the crime scene.

"Nice work," Joe said, "but I had no luck from the cops."

"Well, maybe we should talk to one of our informants?" I asked.

"Good idea," he replied. "I'll call my cousin Sid."

"Tell him to meet us at Waggoner's," I said. "Maybe with a few milkshakes in his stomach, we'll get more information out of him."

The sun was beginning to set as we finally got to the White River Dockyards. It was a long and narrow line of fishing boats, personal luxury ships, and huge wooden crates and boxes on the right side of us where Joe had parked the van. As we walked into the south entrance, the sunset was beautiful, with its pink and purplish hue and the sun with its almost crimson red.

The building which Waggoner's Sports Grill occupied was a 1950s-style bar, which had been converted into a restaurant.

When we got in the door, Sid was waiting for us at the counter. He was already finishing his first milkshake.

"Hey, Sid," called Joe with an Italian accent.

"Hey, Joe," replied Sid with his own Italian accent.

The Vantrice family is Italian-American, with relatives in northeastern America and parts of southern Europe. Some of their ancestors were part of the Italian Mafia, which was how Sid and Joe still had connections in the criminal underworld. Three years before I met them, Joe and Sid were juvenile delinquents who had fallen into the wrong crowd at a young age. They would try to play Robin Hood for their neighbors and get into gang fights for doing so. During one of the gang fights, Jamie, Joe's younger brother, stepped in to protect Joe from a man with a knife and was killed as a result. Joe was left with Jamie dying in his arms as the murderer got away. But after Joe and Sid were both arrested for joyriding in a stolen car and paid three years for the crime in juvenile detention, a reformed Joe vowed to use his skills to help people and make a better life for himself. This was more than I could say about Sid, even though he was one of our best informants.

While Joe and Sid were catching up, I noticed a little boy in a white shirt, khaki shorts, and white tennis shoes, sitting at the drink bar, trying to order a milkshake. When Natasha, one of the cashiers and the older sister of Tommy, the owner of Waggoner's, handed him the milkshake and asked for him to pay for it, the boy looked through his pockets and saw that he didn't have any money.

"I'm sorry, kid," she said, "but unless you've got three dollars, I can't let you have the milkshake."

So, being a good Christian, I decided to help him out.

"It's okay, Natasha," I said, handing her a five-dollar bill. "I'll take care of it."

The boy thanked me silently with a smile. Just as I was about to ask who he was and where his parents were.

"Hey, Leon!" Joe called out.

"Coming, Joe!" I replied, turning my head away for a second.

When I turned back to face the boy, he was gone.

You're welcome, I thought sarcastically, thinking he just went to go sit with his parents.

When I got back to our table, I noticed that Joe had left.

"Hey, Sid, where's Joe?" I asked.

"He had to hit the John for a few minutes," he replied. "Don't worry—he'll be right back."

Sid glanced at a group of leather-clad young men. He then got up from his seat and ran as fast as he could out the back entrance. While this happened, Tommy, the owner of Waggoner's, came out of the kitchen.

"Hey, dumb dumb! Where's our money?" demanded their leader.

"Don't worry, Drac!" Tommy said, his voice trembling. "It's all here!"

"It had better be!" said Drac.

"Yeah, it had better be!" said the smaller one next to him.

"Shut up, Snake!" shouted Drac, punching him in the face.

"Sure, boss," said Snake, wiping a little blood off his face.

"Now, be a *smart* man and hand over your protection payment. Don't want anything to *happen* to this place, right, Tom?"

"No, no, please!" he begged.

Finally, I plucked up the courage to see what was going on.

"Is everything all right, Tommy?" I asked.

"Yeah, everything's fine Leon!" he replied nervously.

Joe came back from the restroom. When he saw the gang, he decided to walk quietly over to our table.

"Hey, Leon! Where did Sid go?" he exclaimed. "Did he bolt before we got all the info we needed?"

"Yes, he did," I said. "But, Joe, I think we need to leave. Like now."

"You know what? I think that's a good idea, bud," he agreed. "Besides, Sid owes me twenty dollars' worth of milkshakes anyway."

"I think that the best way to catch up to is to get to the hippie van and go to your Uncle Roy's house."

"I agree. He always was the kind of guy who would run home to Daddy."

But before we got to the door, that same gang stopped us before we could reach it.

"Going somewhere boys?" asked Drac with an evil smile.

"Hey, man, we don't want any trouble," said Joe.

"Your friend should've thought of that before he stuck his nose in our business!" shouted Drac as his gang started circling us.

"Look, seriously!" I exclaimed. "We really don't want to fight."

"We call ourselves the Scorchers for one reason!" Drac shouted. "Because we burn anyone who gets in our way!"

Then half of them grabbed Joe and took him one way while taking me another. They started beating on us repeatedly. This kept going on until one of them kicked me in the face. The blow broke my nose, which I felt was the last straw. If I were going to save Joe and stop these thugs from beating the tar out of us, I would have to do something that I vowed to never do again.

With the thunderous roar of a lion, I pushed my attackers off of me and got onto my feet. My nose fully healed almost instantly. I then unsheathed my leonine claws from my nailbeds for the first time in a long time. The courage and power of a lion flowed through my veins. My attackers found out very quickly how strong I was as I tossed them thirty feet away like crumpled up pieces of paper. Then I ran over to help Joe. I took down his attackers with ease and helped Joe to his feet.

"Thanks, Leon," he said.

"You're welcome," I replied.

"Wait … how'd you do … look out!" he shouted.

Then just like that, I felt a small pinch on my back. Apparently, Snake had tried to stab me with a knife. I turned around slowly, grabbed him by the neck, and raised him into the air.

"Don't ever do that again!" I roared. "And if I catch you punks bothering the Waggoner's again, you and the rest of Scorchers will be the ones burning, got it?"

"Y-yeah, yeah, I got it!" he said, choking in my grip. Then I dropped him back onto the ground.

I heard the sound of the approaching police sirens.

Although they were five blocks away, I could hear them as if they were right next to me. I realized then that I had caused enough trouble already and that I had to escape. But I couldn't just leave Joe behind—he had suffered enough as far as the law was concerned—so I had no other choice but to take him with me.

"Joe, come on!" I called out. "The police are coming!"

"What are you talking about? I don't hear anything."

"They're five blocks away! Now, come on!"

As we ran outside through the gate and into the alley, I realized that the police sirens were getting louder.

"They're getting closer! Get your arms around my neck!"

"What are you talking about?"

"Just do it!" I shouted, and he jumped onto my back with arms firmly around my neck.

Then, with my strength fueling my legs, I jumped. I can jump distances and heights that are superhuman compared to normal people. After a few jumps to a rooftop a few block away, we managed to escape the police. I set a shaken Joe down off my back. He was more surprised than scared of me, thankfully.

"Okay," he said, panicked, "how in the world did you do all that back there?"

"It's kind of a long story," I said.

"Well, will you please tell me what the heck happened to you for you to take a knife in the back without even flinching?" he exclaimed.

"All right." I sighed. "I guess it's time I told you everything about me."

"When I was two and a half," I began. "My strength as well as the rest of my body was completely normal—until my mom took me with her on a business trip to South Africa."

"A business trip?" Joe asked. "What were you guys doing in South Africa?"

"Well, my mom's a renowned wildlife veterinarian and biologist," I explained. "She was working on a vaccine for a cellular degeneration virus that the local tribes called the dark plague."

"The dark plague?" Joe asked. "Never heard of it."

"My mom told me that it had been killing the local animal population by decaying the living tissue in their bodies at an abnormally fast pace," I continued. "The dark plague caused the deaths of herds of gazelle within two months, while a few herd of elephants would die within six months."

"So it would only be a matter of time before the dark plague would find its way into humans?" Joe exclaimed.

"Yes." I sighed. "Unless my mom, Dr. Amanda Garrett, could find a way to stop it from spreading, but she had been working nonstop for three days with little success. The cells in the test samples just didn't have the strength to make antibodies to survive against it. They would just disintegrate in her microscope."

"But she did eventually find a vaccine for the dark plague, right?" Joe asked.

"Yes, she did." I sighed again. "But not before the accident."

"Accident?" Joe exclaimed. "What accident?"

"Well," I started explaining again, "somehow, a nearby stampede of wildebeests were causing tremors near the camp where my mom was working. She went outside our tent for a minute to see what was happening, but while she was gone, I got fussy and threw one of my toys at a test tube filled with some unknown and an adult male lion's DNA sample that my mom was testing. It spilled and started dripping into my playpen."

"Oh, wow!" Joe exclaimed. "How are you even alive?"

"See, that's the thing!" I exclaimed. "Instead of killing me, both were absorbed into my body while I was crying in my playpen. After she saw what happened, Mom had to pass her work onto a colleague, as we were flown back to the nearest American hospital and were given a clean bill of health and sent home after a couple of hours of observation."

"Wow." Joe was shocked. "Just, wow."

"Can you keep my secret for me?" I asked sternly.

"Leon, do you really think that this is the best time for twenty questions?" Joe asked sarcastically.

"Can you keep my secret?" I asked him again.

Joe saw the seriousness in my eyes.

"All right, I'll keep your secret," he promised while sighing.

We snuck back to the hippie van, and Joe drove me back to my house.

"So see you at the first day back at school tomorrow?" I asked.

"Yeah," Joe said. "See you at school, Leon."

Then as he drove away, I couldn't help but worry about him now that he knew my secret.

The next morning, Annie, Joe, and I were on our way back to another day of classes at Sedalia Central High School.

"Are you nervous?" she asked.

"I am a little," I replied. "What if people make fun of my autism again?"

"Leon, it's okay," Joe reassured me. "You're just as normal as everyone else."

While in class, I started hearing the whispers of some of my classmates talking about Joe's past yet again.

"Isn't that Joe Vantrice?" one of them asked quietly. "I heard he spent three years in juvenile detention because he killed his little brother!"

"I heard that some of his ancestors were part of the Italian Mafia!" another said quietly.

Even though I was annoyed, I kept the situation to myself. But just as the class period ended, I spotted Joe leaving just as the school bell rang.

After school as I stepped on the bus, I decided to sit next to Joe and see how he was feeling. Joe's uncle never let him take the hippie van during school days.

"You really shouldn't sit by me right now, Leon," Joe remarked, slightly annoyed.

"I don't care what people think about you or what they say," I stated. "So you shouldn't either."

"Thanks, partner," Joe said. "I couldn't have asked for a better friend."

"No problem, buddy," I replied.

Then I got settled into my seat.

I sensed danger as the bus came to a screeching stop. The bus was then taken over by criminals trying to escape a gang war that was happening nearby. The bus driver tried to back it up, but then stopped when one of the gang members held him at gunpoint from outside the bus.

"Don't worry, kids," said the bus driver while raising his hands. "Just stay calm."

Then, two members of one of the warring gangs forced the door open and climbed into the bus.

"All right, listen up!" one of them shouted. "If everyone cooperates, no one's gonna get hurt! We're looking for two guys! Once we have them, you'll be free to go!"

Then he saw Annie and took her hostage.

"Hey, pretty lady! You want to be with a hottie like me?" he said, trying to hit on her.

"Get off me, you pig!" Annie screamed, trying to wrestle away from her captor's grip.

"No one burns the Scorchers!" his partner proclaimed as they were escaping with Annie.

I could feel the power and courage of a lion fill my veins once again, along with my anger.

"I have to help her," I said to Joe.

"Go," Joe said. "I'll cover for you."

"Really?" I asked him, surprised. "After everything that's happened?"

"I already lost one brother," Joe said sternly. "I'm not going to lose another."

Realizing he meant every word he said, I pulled my red hoodie over my face to cover my features and stomped a small hole in the metal floor as if it were cardboard.

"Holy mother of crud!" Joe exclaimed as I jumped through the hole and crouched down on all fours underneath the bus.

With the speed, grace, and agility of a jungle cat, I pounced from under the bus, came right behind the kidnapper, and swiped my razor-sharp claws at his face, scratching it before he could react. His partner decided to run away in terror, leaving his partner by himself.

Free of her captor's grip, Annie elbowed him in the chest and ran to safety.

I stood between her and her kidnapper, letting out an almost lion-like growl.

"Take this you little freak!" the gang member shouted as he shot me four times in the chest. But instead of killing me, it felt like four baseballs slamming into my chest. I healed from the bullet wounds within a moment or two and was back on my feet, approaching my would-be killer. I knocked the gun out of his hands and punched him in the chest, sending him flying thirty feet away. I stood next to the bus and gave out another thunderous roar. Both sides of the gang war heard my roar. Most of them tried shooting me, and others tried beating me with baseball bats, but some of them were scared away. They all tried to attack me but were easily defeated thanks to my lion-like powers—superhuman senses, strength, agility, reflexes, endurance, regenerative healing abilities, and razor-sharp retractable claws. When I saw that everyone was safe, I jumped to the side of a nearby building, climbed it, and jumped to the side of another building. By repeating this process several times, I escaped from the police again and made it back home.

CHAPTER 2
WHO IS THE HEAD OF THE DARK CLAW SYNDICATE?

Meanwhile, Drac had managed to evade capture yet again and was hiding in a nearby alley.

"Man!" exclaimed Drac to himself. "I'll never be able to take down that freak in the red hoodie, not with Snake and those other fools!"

"You can't," said a mysterious man, appearing from the shadows and scaring Drac. "Not by yourself, anyway."

"Who are you, punk?" demanded Drac.

"You haven't earned the right to know my real name," said the man. "But you may call me the Mind Breaker."

"All right, so what do you want, Mind-Breaker?" asked Drac mockingly.

"My associates and I would like to offer you a position in our organization," began Mind-Breaker.

"Pass!" Drac scoffed and began to walk away.

"And the power to get your revenge on that, in your words, 'freak in the red hoodie,'" said Mind-Breaker.

At the sound of this, Drac stopped in his tracks and slowly turned around.

"What's the catch?" asked Drac.

"Finally showing some interest, are we?" began Mind-Breaker. "The catch is that you become an agent of our organization and follow our orders exactly as we say."

"Humph!" scoffed Drac.

"So do we have a deal?" Mind-Breaker asked with an evil smile.

"Yeah, we've got a deal," said Drac as they shook hands. "So what kind of power are we talking about here? Guns?"

"Oh," said Mind-Breaker as he injected Drac in the neck with something. "This power is greater than such mortal things!"

"Ugh!" groaned Drac as he collapsed onto the ground. "What did you do to me?" he shouted, almost choking.

"Why, exactly what I promised," Mind-Breaker said casually. "Welcome to the Syndicate, my Human Hydra!"

On the other side of town, completely unaware of the happenings in the alleyway, I had just gotten home after my long, exciting day.

"Hey, Mom, I'm home!" I called out.

But when she came out to greet me, she noticed some dried blood and some holes in my hoodie. She was wearing a black long-sleeved shirt with a green sweater jacket, blue jeans, and white tennis shoes.

"What happened?" she demanded.

"I'm fine," I explained. "I just saved my classmates from a gang war—that's all. Heh, heh."

"It's a miracle that you didn't end up in a hospital or in a funeral home!" she exclaimed sternly.

"Mom, I'm okay. The bullets just left some bruises and made me bleed a little," I reassured her. "Then I healed, just like always. Is it okay if I go to my room to finish the rest of my homework before dinner?"

"Okay." She sighed. "That's fine."

But before I could leave, she stopped me and lifted up my shirt to check me for injuries.

"Mom, I'm fine. Don't worry," I reassured her again.

"Remember, Leon, you're not like most young men," she reminded me. "Please be careful next time."

"Yes, ma'am," I said politely before I went upstairs to my room and after I closed the door. "Man! This is just like the day I discovered my powers and what my parents told me after that incident in front of the whole church in Salemburg!"

Then I started to remember it as if it were yesterday. I was on a soccer team sponsored by the church. I was playing in the last few minutes of the game. The goal was right within sight, but I couldn't get past the opposing team.

"Pass it to me!" I shouted. "I'm open!"

As the ball was coming toward me, I instinctively back flipped into the air and kicked the ball, just like the professional soccer players that I had seen on TV once and made the goal. But when I came back down, I realized that I had just jumped twelve feet into the air and made a small divot in the ground and a hole in the net.

"Oops," I said innocently. "Sorry about that."

I just played it cool and said I had seen it on TV once. Then I just imitated the soccer player using my autism and my eye for detail. But little did I know, it was more than that—much, much more than that.

After the game, I could hear my parents talking about the incident from the kitchen, which was on the other side of our house. They were trying to figure out how to help me.

"How did this happen?" my dad exclaimed. *"Why* did this happen?"

"There's only one possibility, Blake!" my mom said. "The lab accident in South Africa."

"Well, then, how do we *fix* this, Amanda?" he exclaimed. *"How* do we help our son?"

"I don't know!" she finally shouted before she started to cry. "I don't know that I *can* help him."

"I'm sorry, Amanda," he said as he started crying too. "I'm so sorry."

As I sat in my room listening, I was starting to wonder if my parents might send me away to a mad scientist's laboratory somewhere in a foreign country. After they calmed down a few minutes later, my parents came into my room.

"Hey, buddy, how are you doing?" my dad asked.

"I'm fine, sir. What's going to happen?" I asked.

"Well, I'm going to have to call in a couple of favors from my colleagues to keep this situation quiet," he said. "But we are going to have to pay to replace the net and to patch up the divot."

At the sight of me starting to cry, my mom reassured me that everything was going to be fine. But after that, they warned me to not to use my powers and I have kept that vow ever since. That is, until recently.

The next day, Joe and I went over to his Uncle Roy's fighting gym to finish talking to Sid. Even though I didn't want to believe him at the time, Joe claimed that he had another reason for our visit. We found Sid standing on the side of the building with another small group of thugs from the Scorcher gang surrounding him. Sid was dressed in his usual rumpled-up T-shirt, torn-up blue jeans, and scuffed-up white tennis shoes. He had black frizzy hair and blue eyes. He also had a thin, scrawny build, which made him great as a con man, but bad as a fighter.

"Yet another one of his get-rich-quick schemes with the gangs gone horribly awry," I said to Joe, quietly enough so they didn't hear us.

"Aw, give him a break, man," said Joe in the same way. "He's a little misguided is all, just like these guys."

"Excuse me, gentlemen," I addressed them politely. "Would you be so kind as to let our friend go, please?"

"Beat it, fool," said one of the thugs. "We got some business to discuss with this little punk."

"That wouldn't be the kind of business that might have to involve the police, would it?" I asked sarcastically.

"Hey, why don't you back off before we give you a beating!" shouted another one of the thugs.

"Why don't you make us, fool?" asked Joe sarcastically.

"That's it. Let's get them, boys!" shouted the first thug.

Then Joe and I started fighting the thugs, at least for the first few minutes. I heard a shotgun being pumped and instinctively ran over to Joe so that I could keep him from getting hurt. Just after I heard the loud *bang!* of the shotgun, I knew whoever fired it wasn't intending to kill but to intimidate.

Then, as everyone all turned around, there stood Joe's uncle, Roy Vantrice. He was a tall, thin man with white-gray hair, pale skin, and brown eyes. He was wearing a dark red T-shirt, faded blue jeans, and brown shoes. He was holding a twelve-gauge Mossberg shotgun that, from what I could see and smell, had a little bit of smoke and gun oil coming out of the barrel. He was the one who had fired it.

"Unless you boys want to be filled full of lead," started Roy, "get away from my son and his friends, turn around, and go home now!"

"This isn't over, Sid!" one of them said. "Come on, guys, let's go."

Then, they started to turn and walk away from the gym with Roy keeping them at gunpoint until they left.

"Now, will you boys mind explain to me why you're causing trouble again?" he asked.

"We're sorry, Mr. Vantrice," I said. "We were just looking for Sid because he owes us some information."

"Is this true, Joe?" he asked.

"Yes, Uncle Roy. And speaking of whom," Joe said as we saw that he was trying to sneak away.

"Just a minute there, Sid!" I said.

"Aw, come on, guys!" he pleaded. "Give me a break!"

"Where do you think you're going, Sid?" asked Joe sarcastically as we dragged him up against a nearby wall.

"Now listen up, you little rat!" shouted Joe as he grabbed him by his shirt collar. "You owe me money for the milkshakes and some information about Big Daddy Jackson. Now, start talking!"

"All right, all right, all right!" Sid said, panicked. "I'll talk! I'll talk!"

"Why would someone want to target Big Daddy?" I asked.

"I heard a rumor that someone wanted to take over his company," started Sid, "someone from the Dark Claw Syndicate."

"Oh, come on, Sid!" groaned Joe. "Everyone knows that they're just a rumor."

"The Dark Claw Syndicate?" I asked. "What's he talking about?"

"Oh, he's talking about some mysterious new crime syndicate," Joe explained. "Supposedly, they're making big moves in the criminal underworld."

Despite what Joe said, I could tell that Sid was telling the truth thanks to my animal-keen senses.

"What's this person's name?" I asked.

"I don't know the guy's name!" Sid exclaimed. "No one does! But I heard he goes by Mind-Breaker. That's all I know, I swear!"

"All right, Joe, that's enough," I said. "Sid, give Joe his money and call us if you find out anything else."

"Y-yes, will do, Leon," said Sid as he turned and ran away from us.

"Some fools no not what they do," I said, quoting the Bible.

"Scripture, Leon, really?" said Joe sarcastically.

"That's enough, you two," said Roy. "Come on inside if we're going to do this training lesson."

"Training lesson? What's he talking about?" I asked Joe.

"We're going to start some self-defense classes," said Joe, "so that we can protect ourselves in this town."

"What do you mean by *training*, Joe?" I exclaimed. "You know what my parents said: I'm not allowed to use my powers, ever!"

"Oh, relax, Leon," Joe said. "We're just going to work on your technique."

"Oh, okay, I think," I said, believing him in a naive way at first.

"And your temper," he said quietly to himself with a smile.

That would be the last time that I would trust him not to give me a workout.

When we got inside the gym, we went straight into the training room. I saw the white concrete walls were lined with a couple of posters of famous UFC fighters, taught by Roy himself. The light-brown hardwood floors had black and silver weights and barbells scattered around all four corners of the room. On the right side of the room, the whole wall was lined with mirrors that extended to the floor and reached to the edge of the ceiling. On the left side was a line of benches. Exactly in the middle of the room was the fighting ring, where, for the first time in my life, I was scared to use my powers.

"Well, you boys go ahead and start," said Roy. "I'll be in the office watching you train."

"You mean sleeping in your desk chair?" asked Joe sarcastically.

"Have fun and don't kill each other." Roy yawned with a stretch as he walked away to the office and closed the door.

"God, please forgive me for what I'm about to do." I sighed as I stepped into the ring.

"Don't worry about it, Leon," said Joe as he stepped into the opposite side of the ring. "After I'm done training you, you're going to need His help!"

That's when I felt Joe's left fist jab me in the right side of my face. It made me stumble backward into the ropes behind me.

"I don't want to hurt you, Joe," I pleaded with him. "Please don't make me do this!"

"Oh, I'm going to make you do this, Leon," he said. "Now, come at me as hard as you can!"

"No," I said, "I won't hurt you!"

That's when he jabbed me on the left side of my face, knocking me so hard into the ropes that I hung from them, almost in a daze.

"If you don't learn how to control your strength as well as your temper, then you *will* hurt someone eventually," said Joe. "That's why we're training. Now, come on, hit me!"

"No, Joe!" I said. "I'm not going to fight you, let alone hit you!"

"Then you're going to watch everyone you care about die at your hand!" shouted Joe, provoking me. "Your mom, your dad, me, Annie! If you don't learn how to use technique along with your strength and calm down, that's what's going to happen! Now, hit me, you cowardly lion!"

That's when I hit him, landing him flat on the mat, almost knocking him out.

"I'm so sorry, Joe!" I said, almost crying.

"Are you kidding, Leon?" Joe exclaimed. "That was one of the best punches I've felt in a long time!"

"Really?" I exclaimed.

"Yeah!" said Joe. "Now, we just need to work on your technique when you unleash the beast!"

"Seriously, Joe!" I exclaimed. "I could've killed you just now, and you want me to *unleash the beast* on you again?"

"Yes, Leon!" he said. "Because that's how we're going to help you. Now, do it again: unleash the beast!"

Just as he said that, I tried to hit him again, but this time, he blocked it.

"Your wind up makes you too predictable," he said as he shoved me back. "Which can leave you vulnerable to being punched in the gut or flipped over onto your butt. Now, try again."

Then I tried to kick him in the thigh with my right leg, but he grabbed my foot just before I hit him, and I almost got back flipped out of the ring! Thankfully, I landed on my feet just in front of the ropes.

"A little too flashy, Leon," he said. "Try again."

This went on for a couple of hours, including some sparring and running laps around the outside of the gym, until we saw a breaking news bulletin on the nearby TV in Roy's office.

"Sedalia City Police have declared a state of emergency to all residents in the area! According to eyewitness reports, what appears to be a giant humanoid snake with acidic venom has been seen murdering members of the street gang known as the Scorchers. Police advise all residents to stay off the streets and remain in your homes until further notice!" said the newscaster.

"Man, that's one freaky story!" Roy yawned before chuckling. "Are you guys watching some kind of sci-fi movie?"

He then went back to his office to finish his nap.

"Joe, that snake guy's just like me, and he's hurting innocent people!" I exclaimed. "I've got to stop him before he does any more damage!"

"Leon, I don't think that's such a good idea," said Joe. "You barely know how to fight me, let alone whatever that thing is."

"I know, Joe," I said. "But I can't just let whatever that snake thing is do what it wants without facing justice. It's just not right by me."

"All right," said Joe, "but if you're going to do this, you're going to need more than a hoodie to protect yourself and your identity."

Then Joe opened one of the nearby lockers and brought out a custom-made superhero costume. It was a near-skintight jumpsuit made with red leather from where the bottom of the neck met the middle of the collar bone and top of the shoulder blades to just below the pectoral area on the chest and bottom of the shoulder blades, and extended onto both sides of the shoulders. The jumpsuit featured a red leather belt with pouches, with gloves which reached just below the elbows, boots that reached just below the knees, and a red mask.

The forehead, the neck, the lower half of the chest and back, the pants, and the sleeves below the shoulders to the top of gloves were made of a black nylon. It had golden yellow trim on the chin guard, on the pair of green lenses on the mask, and around the border of the golden yellow manes of the golden yellow lion heads that only showed the green eyes and black noses between the pecs in the middle of the chest and on the belt buckle.

"That has to be the most ridiculous thing I've ever seen," I said.

"Oh, come on, Leon!" Exclaimed Joe. "I just finished making you this! You're a superhero, for Pete's sake!"

"No, I'm not Joe," I said. "I'm just trying to help the little guy and protect them from other monsters and beasts—like me."

"Okay," said Joe, "we definitely need to work on your self-image sometime really soon, but right now, don't we have a bad guy to stop?"

"We?" I exclaimed. "Have you lost your mind? You're not coming with me? That thing's way too dangerous!"

"I can take care of myself," said Joe. "Or did you forget that I pretty much kicked your butt today?"

"You're right." I sighed. "I can't believe I'm saying this, but let me suit up."

"All right!" exclaimed Joe. "I was hoping you'd say that!"

"Don't get used to it," I called out as I went to the bathroom to change.

"Whatever, Leoman," Joe called back sarcastically.

After I got changed into the "Leo-Suit," as Joe called it, I looked at myself in the nearby mirror. At first, I felt a little silly. But then, I realized that Joe was right about protecting my family and my identity. So I decided to accept it, despite how I felt. We then went out into the city to find and stop this man-snake-beast-thing whose name we couldn't decide on. Joe took the hippie van and went to question the police officers to find out if there was a connection between the Big Daddy Jackson murder and the attacks from this creature. While I decided to track him from the rooftops using my powers and a unique combination of parkour and free-running that I developed while playing in the zoo exhibits when I was a kid at my mom's work. To be honest, even though I was somewhat rusty, it also felt good to be jumping and running like a jungle cat across the city again. It felt different but great at the same time. I felt free to be the real me.

But as I was starting to enjoy myself. I spotted the snake beast heading down an alley. He had green scales, a head resembling a cobra, and a long tail. He was wearing a torn-up leather jacket, ripped-up blue jeans, and bare feet. I took the opportunity to spy on him, and as I did, I saw him move a dumpster, open a trap door, and run down the stairway to a basement. Even though this all occurred while I was on top of the building across the street, I could see it as if looking through the zoom lens of a camera. I thought at the time that if I didn't go after him, I would lose track of him. So instead of calling Joe for backup, I decided to leap across to the top of the building, then climb down the side of it, and follow close behind him so that he wouldn't get too far away from me.

When I reached the bottom of the dark stairway, I was both amazed and disgusted to find the snake beast was hiding in a secret lab! I could tell that it was an illegal drug lab because of the marijuana plants and some weird white powder that I suspected was heroin, among other exotic plants and powders that I didn't recognize. Thankfully, my healing abilities left me unaffected by the different aromas.

While I was investigating the lab, I heard voices coming toward me from behind a door on the other side of the room. Thinking instinctively,

I hid underneath a table near the trap door entrance. Since the lab had little light coming from the small windows and only a few LED lights on toward the middle of the lab, I knew that whoever they were wouldn't spot me easily. It seemed like two men who were in the middle of an intense argument as they entered the lab.

"Drac, you're an imbecilic fool!" shouted one the men. "Do you have any idea what you've done?"

"Well, sorry, Mind-Breaker!" Drac mocked. "I thought you wanted me to use your little mystery juice to kill that freak in the red hoodie!"

"First, my formula is called FANG," groaned Mind-Breaker. "And second, do any of the gang members you've killed look anything like that so-called hero?"

Mind-Breaker was wearing a dark violet trench coat and a dark violet hood to cover his face. Other than that, he was wearing a black business suit along with black gloves and shoes.

"So I killed a few people. Big deal!" shouted Drac. "You wanted me to get his attention, and now we've got it!"

Mind-Breaker raised his hand and made a grabbing motion, which made Johnson start gasping for air as if someone were choking him to death.

"You idiot!" shouted Mind-Breaker. "You've exposed yourself to the public eye, and now this entire operation is in jeopardy!"

"I'm sorry … sorry …" gasped Drac.

After hearing his apology, Mind-Breaker released him with a wave of his hand. Drac then began to gasp and cough as new air filled his lungs.

"I gave you this power of the Human Hydra." Mind-Breaker sighed. "Don't make me take it away!"

While all this was going on, I peeked out from under the table and found a vial with a glowing yellowish-green liquid. This must have been a sample of the FANG drug that they were fighting about. Seizing the opportunity, I snatched the vial and tried to make a quiet escape. Unfortunately, I banged my head on the table, causing it to tip over while trying to climb out from underneath it.

"Hey, it's him!" Johnson shouted as he spotted me.

"Well, what are you waiting for, an invitation?" said Mind-Breaker. "Kill him and get that sample back, now!"

"All right. Yes, boss," said Drac, annoyed.

As Drac started to chase after me up the stairway, I saw Mind-Breaker sneak away out of the corner of my eye. Just as I made it out of the lab, he tripped me up by grabbing my leg. I instinctively reacted by rolling onto my back and kicking him off me. At first, I thought that he broke his back as he slammed into a brick wall. But when I went to go check on him, I was shocked to see that there were five duplicates that looked just like him.

"What in the world?" I said.

"Surprised, you little freak?" He and his duplicates snickered. "Well, guess what? That's not the only thing I can do!"

He and his clones then blasted me with acidic venom from his mouth that burnt my arms along with parts of my chest and face as I attempted to block it.

"Aaaahhhh!" I groaned with pain.

Even though I had experience with similar reptilian poisons, this poison was different—much more potent—which made my body's attempts at recovering from the pain and healing from it harder than usual. Miraculously, I managed to escape by grabbing the nearby dumpster and slammed it into them, stunning them for a minute or two and then leaping a couple of blocks away to a nearby rooftop and then running across the rooftops to get away.

"You can't escape me that easily, you little runt!" he called out after he regained his focus. "I will hunt you down, and I will kill you!"

I caught up with Joe across the city as he finished talking to Mr. Jacobs on the phone.

"Joe," I called out as I started passing out.

"Hey Leon, I … Leon!" he said, shocked at my injuries.

Joe caught me in his arms, and he was calling my mom just before I finally passed out.

CHAPTER 3
WHAT WILL LEON CHOOSE?

The next thing that I knew, I woke up on an examination table to my mom tending to my injuries to help speed up my recovery.

"Mom, where am I?" I asked weakly.

"Shush," she said quietly. "It's okay, sweetie. You're in my lab. Joseph already told me what happened."

"I'm sorry that I didn't tell you sooner and that I broke my promise," I apologized. "I thought that I could take him on by myself, but I ended up getting my butt kicked instead."

"Leon, I'm not mad at you for using your abilities," she said. "I'm proud that you're using them to help others, just like your father and I taught you."

"Thanks, Mom," I said. "For this and for understanding."

"But you are grounded until we stop this Human Hydra, as Joseph mentioned," she said.

"But Mom!" I exclaimed, "the Masquerade Dance at school is tonight!"

"Don't argue with your mother!" said my dad as he came in.

"Sorry, Dad," I said. "It's good to see you, sir."

"You're both lucky not to be seriously harmed or in handcuffs," he said firmly. "Your mother also said that she had evidence in connection to Big Daddy Jackson's murder?"

"Yes, dear," Mom said. "The acid that was used to brand his forehead, kill the gang members, and burn Leon is made of the same biochemical composition."

"All right," he said. "I'll put out an APB for this Human Hydra guy."

"Let me help too, Dad," I pleaded.

"No, Leon," he said firmly. "You need to rest, and you're still grounded from going to the dance. Do you understand?"

"Yes, sir," I said obediently.

It was a shame that I couldn't go because Annie and I were going to cosplay as Belle and the Beast from the Disney movie.

The worst part was I had to call and lie about why I couldn't go the dance tonight. As I pressed the send button on my phone, my disappointment turned to dread as she answered her phone.

"Hello?" she answered.

"Hey, Annie," I sighed.

"Hey, Leon," she greeted me, concerned. "Are you okay?"

"Yeah," I replied. "It's just …"

I took a deep breath before I let out a big sigh.

"I can't go to the dance tonight," I replied.

"What?" she exclaimed. "Why?"

"Because." I sighed. "My parents want me to stay home and clean up a mess I made today."

"Oh, okay," she replied. "I was really looking forward to seeing you tonight, though."

That's when my heart dropped into my stomach—because I felt so bad about not being able to see her and tell her how I felt about her.

"Yeah, me too," I finally replied.

"Well, I have to go get ready." She sighed. "Good luck cleaning up your mess."

"Annie?" I asked nervously.

"Yes, Leon?" she asked.

I thought about telling her right then and there on the phone. But I decided not to. Besides, if she found about my leonine powers or anything to do about me being a superhero, she'd either laugh at me or run away in fear and loathing.

"I hope you have fun at the dance tonight," I replied.

"Thanks, Leon." She sighed. "I hope to see you at school next week."

"Same here," I replied. "Well, I better get to cleaning. See you around, Annie."

"You too, Leon," she replied. "Bye."

"Bye," I said before I hung up the phone.

It was one of the worst phone calls I had ever made.

When I got home an hour later, Mom sent me to my room to rest. But as I laid my head down on my pillow, I couldn't help but feel stressed and worried about both situations. First, I had to find Human Hydra and stop him from taking more innocent lives. Then I thought about how mad Annie was going to be for ditching her. I didn't know how I was going to explain this, especially since I'd been thinking about telling her how I felt about her. I'd always felt this strange and mysterious connection between Annie and me, as if the hands of God drew us together to each other. Even when we first met, no matter where I went or how far away I was, she always drew me back to her like a breath of fresh air. It seems I took every chance to be close to her, without hesitation or forethought, to my embarrassment. Because of this, I was torn between being a hero, or being a young man in love.

So, after a lot of thought, I decided to be a young man in love. After I checked the house and found my parents were still away, I grabbed my Beast costume, snuck out of the house, and leapt my way to school.

When I got to school, the Masquerade Dance was already in full swing, so I landed on the concrete roof of the school and checked to see if anyone from school security had seen me. When the coast was clear, I changed into my costume with the cool breeze sending a chill throughout my body as I did so. Afterwards, I leapt down from the roof, walked up from the side of the school, and checked in at the main entrance.

"Hey Leon," said Sid. "Beast from the Disney movie, huh? Nice."

"Nice to see you too, Sid," I said. "Is Annie here tonight?"

"Maybe, for five bucks?" said Sid with an outstretched hand.

"Really, Sid?" I said. "You're such a conman."

After I got inside, I saw that the school's cafeteria had been converted into a dark Victorian era–themed ballroom. The tables were pushed to sides of the long and narrow cafeteria to make room for the dance floor, which had a row of chandeliers above it. There were candelabras with a single rose as centerpieces on each table. Since it was a masquerade dance, there were people dressed up as the Phantom from the *Phantom of the Opera*, among other characters. For once in my life, I felt as if I wasn't the only one wearing a mask.

I tried looking for Annie with no luck. I saw that Joe was DJing for the dance and decided to ask him for help.

"Hey, Joe, how are you doing?" I asked.

"Hey, Leon, how are you feeling?" he asked.

"Everything's healed up," I said. "Have you seen Annie tonight?"

"Yeah, she's over by the drink table in the yellow Belle dress," he said. "She was asking about you earlier."

I felt my heart skip a beat for a second.

"Oh, really?" I asked. "Thanks for telling me, Joe."

"No problem," he said. "Have fun—within reason."

As I started walking toward her, I started thinking about how beautiful she looked in that dress. If I had a picture of Belle from the movie and compared it to Annie, I would've thought that the animators of the movie had made drawings of her to make Belle. She's a lot like the character too. Strong, independent, intelligent, beautiful—A breath of fresh air and compassionate in every sense. Then I began to remember the day we first met.

It was the second month after my family, and I moved to Sedalia City. Being a Christian family, we decided to visit a local church during a choir practice on a Wednesday night. My parents had told the pastor that I could sing very well, and while this may have been true, despite how I felt about singing in front of new people, my parents insisted that

I should try out for a solo. Even now, I can remember during the tryouts that there was another family who wanted their daughter to try out for a solo as well. So we both tried out for the same song, and somehow, managed to get both of our solos turned into a duet. We became best friends and are now at the same school dance over a year later.

"Hey, Annie," I said dreamingly.

"Hi, Leon," she said. "Are you okay?"

"Uh, yes. I'm fine," I stammered as I broke out of my trance of blank staring. "You look very pretty in that yellow ballroom dress. Just like Belle from the movie."

"Aw, thank you. You look nice too," she replied. "I thought you had to clean up a mess at your house."

"Huh?" I asked. "Oh, yeah. I got it cleaned up earlier than I thought. So Mom and Dad let me come."

Suddenly, the "Beauty and the Beast" song from the Disney movie came on the speakers.

I glanced at Joe and mouthed the words, "What are you doing?"

"Just dance with her!" he mouthed back as he shrugged his shoulders.

"So, Annie, would you like to dance?" I asked as I turned my gaze back to her.

"Yes, I would love to," she replied.

So I took her outstretched hand and led her onto the dance floor.

As I danced with her, I thought about how she said she'd "love to" dance with me. Did that mean she felt the same way about me? Or was she just doing it to be nice to me? Either way, it was nice, possibly even romantic.

"Annie?" I asked.

"Yes, Leon?" she asked back.

"I … I just want you to know that—" I stammered.

"Leon, I know what you're going to say, and—" she said as we were about to embrace into a kiss.

But as we did, someone kicked the door open. We all looked with surprise and saw that it was the Human Hydra guy whom I fought before as Leoman. He made his presence known by tossing aside three grown men like ragdolls.

"All right, you lion-costume-wearing freak!" he shouted. "Come on out unless you want to see these people melted like ice in hot water!"

That's when I realized he was looking for me.

"Aw, man!" I whispered. "He must've tracked me by the residue on my skin!"

"Wait, what are you talking about?" Annie asked me.

Since I just noticed that Annie was still standing right next to me, I quickly decided to make something up.

"Uh, nothing," I replied. "Maybe I should call my dad about this."

Human Hydra fired a stream of his venom into a corrosive half circle a few feet in front of him. This, unfortunately, caused all the students and faculty to panic and start running away in all directions. However, it also gave me an opportunity to sneak away from the crowd and change into something that would protect my identity. I hated to do it, but I had to ditch Annie to make a costume change.

"Annie, run for the nearest exit and don't look back!" I told her.

"What're you going to do?" she asked.

"I'm going to call my dad!" I told her.

As she ran away into the crowd, I gave her one last longing glance, hoping that someday I could explain everything.

After Annie made her escape, Joe and I met up in the crowd and discussed a plan.

"So we found our perp. Now what?" I asked.

"Now, we need Leoman," said Joe seriously as he pulled out a newly repaired version of the costume with the same color scheme as before.

"Wait a darn minute. I thought that it was destroyed the last time?" I said.

"Your dad and I made some upgrades while you were knocked out," said Joe quietly. "This suit has a thin layer of insulated Kevlar and Nomex. He won't burn through this one.

"What's with the gun?" I asked as I noticed there was some form of handgun that he brought along with it.

"Relax, Leon," Joe reassured. "It's a tranquilizer gun filled with a formula your mom made to knock him out."

"All right, Joe," I said.

I ran into the nearby restroom to quickly change into the new suit. As I looked into the bathroom mirror, I realized that when I wore this costume, I was not my usual self but someone else, something else—Leoman. A few minutes later, I emerged out the bathroom and ran back into the dance hall and gave out a thunderous roar that echoed in every corner of the room. Human Hydra turned to face me with a sadistic smirk on his face.

"Who're you supposed to be?" he asked sarcastically.

"Leoman," I stated confidently. "Now, you want me, here I am."

"I wouldn't be so sure about that, runt," he said.

One of his copies came in with Annie as his hostage!

"Let go of me, you creep!" she demanded, trying to break free of his grip.

His copy shoved her into his grip.

"Let her go, Drac!" I shouted with a growl.

"I'm Human Hydra now, you little freak!" he shouted. "And unless you want the little lady here to be disintegrated by my venom, you'll fork over that vial you stole from my boss!"

"Why, so he can make more monsters like you?" I asked sarcastically.

"The time for talking is over, runt!" he shouted. "Make your choice, the vial, or your little girlfriend!"

After I thought about it for a few seconds, I decided to use a risky option of using the tranquilizer gun. I might've been able to shoot him in the arm with the new formula that might depower him, but I would also run the risk of hurting Annie if I missed, so I had no choice but to take the risk. If Human Hydra were holding onto Annie, he could snap her neck with one movement.

"Time's up, runt," he said. "Make your choice now, because we both know you don't have the power to stop me!"

"I already have," I said.

Instinctively, I grabbed the gun from the right hip holster and shot at Human Hydra quick-draw cowboy style, praying that the dart would hit him instead of Annie. Miraculously, it did. I managed to shoot him in the shoulder just to the side of Annie's head. The force of the impact managed to make him drop to the ground, and he released his grip on Annie when she elbowed him in the chest.

"Run, Annie!" I said.

"But wait, who are you?" she asked, beginning to freak out.

"Do it now!" I shouted, almost roaring.

"Okay!" she screamed as she started to run away.

I felt horrible for shouting at her like that, but I had no choice if it was going to save Annie's life. Then I realized that Human Hydra had a weakness. His copy began to disintegrate, and he was getting back up. But at the same time, he was staggering, possibly weakened from the formula.

That's when I decided to take advantage of the situation. I ran over to him and started to "unleash the beast," as Joe had taught me.

"You don't get it, do you?" I shouted as I began a flurry of punches. "Just because you now have power doesn't mean you get to do what you want with it! For years, I was afraid of my power and how if I wasn't careful, I could easily kill innocent people! You chose to hurt them. Now I choose to protect them!"

"W-why?" he said weakly

"Because God didn't just give me the courage and power of a lion," I replied. "He gave me the gentle and compassionate heart of a human to be kind and care about others before myself."

Before I left the dance, I tried to apologize to Annie.

"It's okay," she said. "Thank you for saving my life."

"Thank you for understanding," I said with a growl to disguise my voice.

I heard police sirens approaching the dance hall as I decided to make my exit. The police came and took Drac, who had just turned back into his human form thanks to Mom's antidote. Annie's parents came and took her home while Joe and Rachel relayed the story to the police and to Mr. Jacobs, who made sure that they got their reward. Everyone was safely on their way back home for the night, so I decided it was time for me to go home too.

As I made it back to my house after the dance, I saw that all the lights were off. Feeling confident that my parents were unaware that I left, I entered through my bedroom window. Suddenly, the lights flashed on in the room, and there stood my mom in the doorway.

"You deliberately disobeyed your father and me!" she shouted.

"I'm sorry that I went to the dance, Mom," I said calmly, "but I did stop the Human Hydra before he could hurt anymore people."

"Yes, but at the risk of Annie's life!" she shouted.

"How do you know that?" I exclaimed.

"Annie's friend, Rachel, was at the dance. She posted a video on Facebook, along with an article and a photo to the *Sedalia Star*!" she shouted.

I watched with shock as my mom showed me a video of my fight from earlier that night, along with the risky shot I took to save Annie's life.

"I can't believe she did that!" I exclaimed.

"I can't believe that you, of all people, would risk an innocent life like that!" my dad shouted just as he got home.

"Dad, I'm sorry," I said. "I know that it was a risky shot, but if I didn't take it, she would've died."

"I know, Leon," Dad said. "But you shouldn't take such a risk unless you can avoid it."

"Yes, sir," I said sadly.

"But you did what you had to stop him," he said. "For that, we are proud of you."

"Thanks, Dad," I said, relieved. "But I was hoping to ask you guys for something."

"What is it, son?" Mom asked.

"I was hoping to ask for your blessing to continue being Leoman," I said.

"I don't know if we can," said Dad before I interrupted him.

"Please, Dad," I begged. "There are bad guys out there that the SCPD can't handle them by themselves."

"Leon—" said Mom, before I interrupted her too.

"Mom, you know that Leoman can," I said sternly. "You both know that I can."

After a moment of silence, my parents made their decision.

"All right, son," Dad said, "You can be Leoman."

"Yes!" I shouted happily.

"But, Leoman must obey the law," said Dad, "and work with the police."

"Yes, sir," I said obediently.

And so began my other life, my heroic life, my life as Leoman!

But as my family and I celebrated the rise of Leoman at our house, something evil was taking place at the county jail, while the guards were unaware and Drac was waiting in a jail cell pending his trail.

"Drake Johnson!" shouted a guard. "Your lawyer's here!"

"I didn't ask for one!" said Drac from his jail cell.

"Oh, I think you did," said the familiar sinister voice of Mind-Breaker.

"Mind-Breaker," whispered Drac. "Hey, look, boss, I can explain everything."

"Oh, I know everything I need to know!" he said angrily.

He made the same choking gesture with his hand, and Drac started gasping for air all over again.

"You have failed me!" he said. "And I do not tolerate failure!"

"Please, boss … give me another chance!" Drac gasped.

"No, I think not," he said.

He clenched his choking hand into a fist, this action caused Drac slumped back onto the ground into a coma, his mind broken at the hands of the Mind-Breaker.

"Well, so much for that experiment," he said passively. "Now that I have Mr. Jackson's chemical plant, it's time to work on my other ones."

CHAPTER 4
WHAT IS A K-BOMB?

It had been a week since I fought the Human Hydra, and I felt like all I had done was stop a few muggings, when I should've been going after this mysterious Mind-Breaker guy that he was talking to. But instead of doing that, I was at an outdoor presentation in Sedalia City Park with Joe, reporting about some up and coming demolitions expert who had found a new way to blow stuff up. Uh, hello? They're called explosives, and they've already been invented.

"Oh, come on, Leon, lighten up," said Joe as he noticed the look on my face.

"Maybe I could, if we knew who that Mind-Breaker guy was," I said, annoyed.

"All right, Leon," Joe said, "I know that you're worried about him, but for now we can only take one day at a time and hope that he slips up soon."

"You're right, I'm sorry, Joe," I said.

"It's okay, bud," Joe said. "Hey, the presentation's about to start."

"I'll make sure to get some good shots," I said, taking out my camera.

"Ladies and gentlemen," began the announcer. "Introducing the man behind the latest innovation in demolitions technology, Dr. John Kingston!"

The scientist, Dr. John Kingston, was a relatively short and overweight man who appeared to be in his midforties, with thinning dark brown hair along with a sparse beard and mustache and a pale complexion that had a reddish hue from being in the sunlight too long. He was wearing a dark red sweater vest over a light blue button-up shirt, which was mostly covered by an unbuttoned white lab coat, a pair of light tan pants, and dark brown shoes.

"Welcome to the presentation. Thank you, everyone!" he said. "Before I begin, I would like to thank the mayor of Sedalia Bay, Dave Early, for his funding of my invention, and the Baker Chemical Factory for the supplies needed to make my invention possible. For the last five years, I have been working on an invention that will render all forms of demolition technology obsolete."

He pulled out a small, metallic device the size and shape of a soda can out of his pocket, which everyone thought was a grenade, making their eyes widen with fear, and a few of them gasped in terror at first.

"No, no, don't be alarmed, everyone," he said reassuringly. "This is my invention, the kinetic energy emitter—or, as I like to call it, the K-Bomb."

This was met with a light applause as everyone was still unsure of the device. As I was taking photos of the device, I heard the voice of someone whom I hadn't suspected would be here.

"This isn't going to end well," he said quietly.

I turned my head and saw it was the boy in white from that night in Waggoner's Sports Grill.

"Hey, how'd you get in here?" I asked.

"He's playing with forces that he cannot hope to control," he said. "You need to get these people out of here, Leon."

"Wait a minute. How do you even know my name?" I asked, surprised.

"Hey, Leon," Joe whispered. "Who are you talking to?"

"I'm talking to the little boy in white over here," I said, turning my gaze to Joe for a split second.

"What little boy?" asked Joe.

When I turned my head back to face the boy, he had disappeared again.

"I'm telling you, he was right there," I said.

"Right," said Joe sarcastically. "We'll have to ask your mom to get your eyes checked later."

By the time I refocused on Dr. Kingston, he was about to begin to demonstrate the K-Bomb.

"Perhaps this will ease your minds, fellow citizens," he said. "Please bring out example A!"

A group of construction workers brought a pallet of bricks stacked as a section of a brick wall onto the stage. He walked over to the pallet, placed the K-Bomb on the top row of the brick wall, activated it, and ran back to the other side of the stage.

"As you can see, ladies and gentlemen," he explained. "After ten seconds of building up a charge, the K-Bomb has emitted a localized electrical energy field that has vaporized the brick wall beneath it, without it or the pallet being vaporized in the process."

With a small *clunk*, the K-Bomb fell onto the pallet, and the energy field dissipated. After it dissipated, the audience erupted in applause.

"Thank you very much, everyone," he said as the applause started to die down. "Would you like to see some more?"

"Yeah!" said some of them as the audience applauded again.

"Very well," he said. "Please bring out examples B and C!"

The same group of construction workers bought two more pallets. The first was a stack of wooden two-by-fours, stacked four rows high by four rows, side by side. The second was a steel plate shaped into a square and standing up on one end. He walked over to the first pallet and repeated the same process he had done with the pallet of bricks, and it vaporized the two-by-fours without harm to the pallet underneath. But when the doctor pressed the button again to vaporize the steel plate, it instead fizzled and popped uncontrollably. As the crack finally broke open, the energy burned the doctor's hand, accidently making it blast out wildly like lightning in different directions when he dropped it.

The audience started panicking and ran in every direction, trying to get away from the blasts. Realizing that no one else could stop the K-Bomb without getting killed, I took the opportunity to sneak away from the action to change into the Leo-Suit and become Leoman in the park's restroom. After doing so, I ran back to the presentation, passing by onlookers running the other direction and leapt onto the stage. By then, the K-Bomb had become so unstable that, in addition to the blasts, it looked like it was about to explode. Thinking quickly, I ran over to the K-Bomb, grabbed it, and began crushing it to stop it from blasting while using my body to shield people from the aftermath of the small explosion of electrical energy. I managed to survive being electrocuted with only moderate burns and bruises on my chest just before I passed out.

I woke up in the hospital to Joe calling my name.

"Hey, wake up, tough guy," he said. "How are you doing?"

"Where am I?" I asked.

"You're in the hospital," he said. "Don't worry; I managed to get the suit off you before the ambulance picked you up."

"Thanks, Joe," I said. "I owe you one."

"Hey, don't worry about it, bud," he said.

My mom came rushing in.

"Leon?" she said panicking. "Oh, honey, are you all right?"

"Yeah, I'll be all right, Mom," I said. "Where's Dad?"

"He's at a City Hall meeting with the mayor and the commissioner about the K-Bomb incident," she said.

Annie walked in.

"Hey, is everyone all right?" she asked.

"Yeah, we're fine," I said.

"Good, I came as soon as I heard," she replied. "What happened?"

My mom and Joe told her about the K-Bomb incident. After a long and somewhat awkward silence between us, I asked Mom and Joe to give us some time to talk privately. After they left, I tried to apologize for abandoning her during the Human Hydra attack, but she spoke first.

"I can't believe you just left me at the dance!" she said angrily.

"I know. I'm sorry," I said. "But Dad put out an APB on that Human Hydra guy, so I had to call him in."

"I don't care! Your dad is the police, not you!" she said. "You left me there scared and alone!"

"Well, sometimes the police need informants, don't they?" I said, frustrated. "Besides, we both got out of there safe and sound."

"That's not the point, Leon! Informants are trained, and you're only human!" she exclaimed. "And I don't know what I would do if you died!"

She broke into tears and ran out the door.

"Annie!" I called out. "Please, come back," I secretly begged quietly to myself.

"Well, that went well," said Joe sarcastically as he and my mom came back in the door.

"Stop teasing him, Joseph," said my mom. "Are you all right, Leon?"

"Yeah, Mom," I said sadly. "I'll be okay."

"Aw, cheer up, bud," said Joe. "The good news is the doctor said you'll be out of here soon."

"Yay!" I exclaimed.

"The bad news is," said my mom, "the hospital needs to run a few blood tests to make sure that everything's okay."

"Boo!" I exclaimed.

"Oh, come on, Leon," Joe said sarcastically. "Don't tell me you're afraid of needles."

"I'm not afraid of them," I exclaimed. "I just flat out hate them!"

The person whom I dreaded to see at times like this came walking in the door with a syringe in his hand.

"Hello, Leon," said Dr. Scott Paxton, our family doctor. He was a tall, thinly-built man with a graying black hair and mustache. He had a dark tan complication and was wearing a light blue button up shirt, tan dress pants, and brown shoes.

"Doc, don't you dare stick that needle in my arm!" I exclaimed.

"Oh, come now, Leon," he said, trying to comfort me. "You're an abnormally strong young man, and you heal faster than normal people. Do we really need to go through this every time?"

"Yes," I exclaimed, "because you're not putting that needle in my arm!"

"Wait a minute," said Joe. "How does he know about Leon's powers?"

"Dr. Paxton is an old friend and my colleague since medical school," said my mom.

"Doc, you stick that needle in my arm, and I'm going to punch you through the wall!" I exclaimed.

"Hey, Leon," said Joe, "Annie's back."

"What?" I asked, losing focus for a second.

I felt that same painful pinch that I always do every time I get stuck with a needle.

"Oooooowwwwwwww!" I hollered so loud that the whole hospital could hear me.

While I was dealing with the recent heartache and pain in my arm, my dad was at city hall in the office of Mayor Dave Early, watching silently as the mayor grilled Dr. Kingston about the K-Bomb incident earlier in the park.

"What were you thinking, Kingston?" shouted the mayor.

"Well, I'm sorry, Mr. Mayor," said Dr. Kingston.

"Sorry, doesn't cut it!" shouted my dad. "Several people got hurt in those explosive blasts, including my son! Who's going to pay for his stay in the hospital?"

"Now, now, Chief Garrett," said Dr. Kingston apologetically. "I know that what happened was a mishap, but with a little more research and testing—"

"Research and testing?" shouted the mayor. "You must be crazy to think that I'm going to let you continue those dangerous experiments of yours in my city!"

"But, Mr. Mayor," said Dr. Kingston. "I can assure you that there won't be a repeat of what happened today."

"You better believe that for certain," shouted the mayor, "because I'm not letting you continue your K-Bomb experiments in my city! I'm shutting you down!"

"No, no, please!" pleaded Dr. Kingston. "Please, I'm begging you. This is my life's work. Years of hard work and research just thrown away like yesterday's trash!"

"It's over, Dr. Kingston," said the mayor. "You're never working in this city again!"

"No! No!" shouted Dr. Kingston as he was being dragged out of the mayor's office. "I'm ruined! Ruined! You'll pay for this, Dave Early! I swear to you, you will pay!"

After Dr. Kingston was thrown out onto the sidewalk outside of city hall, he got up, dusted off his clothes, and stopped by a local bar to drown his sorrows before he spent the whole day as he walked all the way back home across the city in disgrace.

After a few hours of observation, the hospital finally discharged me so I could go home and rest up for school the next day. When the next day finally arrived, I was back in school. At the time, I figured that, thanks to Leoman, this whole K-Bomb business was over with—especially since Dad told me what had happened in the mayor's office just before I left the house for school.

Poor Dr. Kingston, I thought.

I couldn't even imagine what it must be like to work so hard on something just to have it, quite literally, blow up in your own face. Then I tried to imagine what it must be for his son, Bobby. I mean, the last time I had heard, Dr. Kingston had used a lot of his own money to fund his invention. Now, with his experiments and his dreams up in flames, it looked as if they both were going to lose everything.

How right I would find out to be when I saw Bobby come walking off the bus, smiling with false glee to cover up the feelings of disappointment and rage I could see burning in his eyes. He was a small, skinny young man who was a year younger than me. He had red hair and blue eyes and was wearing a green T-shirt, blue jeans, and white tennis shoes. I tried to approach him with compassion, when I was shoved out of the way by a former friend turned resident Gaston from Disney's *Beauty and the Beast.*

"So, Bobby!" Hector Ross said loudly. "When's your dad going to come up with another crazy invention? Ha, ha, ha!"

"Well, I don't talk about my dad right now," Bobby said, looking downcast.

"What's the next one going to do?" he said jokingly. "Blow up the whole city? Ha, ha, ha!"

"Shut up, Hector," Bobby said quietly.

"Oh, what do you think you're going to do, Woods?" He laughed loudly.

"I said shut up!" Bobby shouted just before punching Hector in the face. "I'm a better man than my father will ever be! Do you hear me? Ever!"

"All right, all right—that's enough!" said Mr. Matthews, the school's business teacher, as he came to break up the fight.

"He started it!" said Bobby.

"Well, I'm ending it!" said Mr. Matthews. "Now, both of you, to the principal's office!"

One of the secretaries who works in the main office came up to Mr. Matthews and handed him a piece of paper.

"All right, listen up," Mr. Matthews announced, "Leon Garrett, Joe Vantrice, Annie Jones, and Rachel Peters, go to the main office to sign out for your internship, please."

"All right, Mr. Garrett," said Mr. Matthews just before leaving with Bobby and Hector. "You heard me, now go on."

"Yes, thank you, sir," I said politely.

When Dr. John Kingston finally got home, the sun was beginning to set into nighttime. He noticed a "foreclosure" notice on the front door of his house. He grabbed it, ripped it in half, and tossed it aside with an angry grunt. He went into the house, which was a total wreck to begin with from the dirty clothes and trash that laid everywhere throughout the house, because he was always too busy or too tired to clean it up himself or to make his son do it.

His son, Bobby Woods, was adopted by Dr. Kingston's wife, Mary, when he was just a baby. He has been a rebellious fifteen-year-old with a childlike love for the character ever since she used to read the stories of Peter Pan and his adventures before she died when Bobby was just five years old. When Dr. Kingston came into the living room and saw his son laying on the couch while reading one of his Peter Pan books yet again, he snatched it out of his son's hands and threw it across the room in a fit of rage.

"What did I say about reading such a childish book?" Dr. Kingston said.

"Why do you care?" asked Bobby sarcastically. "You've never had any other interest besides that K-Boom thing or whatever it is."

"Don't you dare make fun of my life's work!" said Dr. Kingston, grabbing his son angrily and bringing him inches between their faces.

Seeing the familiar look of rage in his father's eyes, he had great fear; he was out of line and should be silent for his sake of health.

"I'm sorry, Dad," said Bobby. "I was just kidding. How was your day, sir?"

"My day? Haven't you seen the news on TV?" shouted Dr. Kingston. "Forget it! I'm going to the lab. Don't bother waiting up on me!"

Walking out the back of the house and slamming the screen door, Dr. Kingston weaved his way through the overgrown grass and decaying leaves, stepping on the occasional broken glass beaker or shaking of a ragged plastic bag that managed to get caught on his shoe. The lab resided in an old tool shed, its wooden structure deteriorating from rot and the slowly creeping mildew. The inside of the tool shed was dark, with the only place in the lab that was clean and organized was a long, thin wooden table that contained the secrets to creating his K-Bomb invention.

"All my life, I've worked to create this failed invention of mine," said Dr. Kingston to himself. "And now it's all for nothing because of that cowardly mayor!"

Feeling like there was nothing left for him in the world, Dr. Kingston attempts to do the unthinkable. First, he turned on the power source for the K-Bomb, known as an ECD (or energy-conversion device), which takes any form of energy from a certain radius around itself and turns it into electrical energy, which it can use to charge itself or power other devices. Second, he fills an unfinished K-Bomb with energy to the point of overloading it. And finally, as the device is sparking and crackling with energy, he grasps it and holds to the middle of his chest as it builds up with energy.

"So long to this idiot-ridden world, and good riddance!" he shouted as his final words as the K-Bomb finally exploded.

But, instead of seeing the sight of angels greeting him in the afterlife, all that the good doctor saw was him surrounded by burning wood and scorched earth, his lab leveled from the explosion. Miraculously, he had managed to survive the explosion without harm to himself or his clothing. If that wasn't strange enough, his body was crackling with the same electrical energy he used to fuel the K-Bomb that should've killed him, but all the doctor felt at first was puzzled and an odd tingling sensation throughout his body.

How in the world did I survive? he thought. *That K-Bomb should've disintegrated me like it did during the presentation!*

As he was trying to figure that out, he suddenly heard Bobby's panicked voice as it came running toward him.

"Dad? Dad!" Bobby shouted. "Are you okay?"

"What? Yes!" Dr. Kingston replied. "Yes, I'm fine."

"What happened to your lab?" asked Bobby.

"Oh, it just blew up," said Dr. Kingston passively. "A minor setback."

"A minor setback?" said Bobby, surprised. "You could've died in there!"

"That was the general idea!" shouted Dr. Kingston. "Now, leave me alone!"

"But, Dad," said Bobby, shocked. "You need to go to the hospital!"

"I said *leave me alone*!" Dr. Kingston screamed as he finally released his first wave of electrical energy from his body, which blasted in all directions and knocked Bobby off his feet.

Surprised at what he had just done, Dr. Kingston realized that not only did his K-Bomb failed to kill him, but it also gave him the power of a C4 explosive, which he tested on a nearby broken beaker, which shattered second after he blasted at it. After lighting a bush on fire with his newfound powers, he decided to use to get his revenge on the mayor of Sedalia City, not caring for anyone who got in his way. As he started away on his path of destructive vengeance.

"Please, Dad," pleaded Bobby as he grabbed his father's pant leg. "Please, don't do this, Dad—I beg you."

"Get off me!" shouted Dr. Kingston as he kicked his son off him. "It's time to grow up, you useless brat!"

As his father walked away for the last time in a fit of rage, Bobby's heart and mind were finally shattered as the years of abuse finally took their toll. That night, Bobby vowed he would never let any other child be abused the same way as he was. That night, he vowed never to trust any adult or anyone in authority. That night, he vowed to do something that would make him a hero in the eyes of every single child who had been orphaned or abused.

I'll show you, Dad, he said to himself. "I promise you, I'll show you!"

CHAPTER 5
WHAT HAS BECOME OF DOCTOR KINGSTON?

An hour after we made it back into the newspaper offices of the *Sedalia Star*, Joe, Annie, Rachel, and I were rushed into Mr. Jacobs's office again to receive another pair of assignments.

"All right boys and girls listen up!" he said. "You did well with your last assignments, but those two reporters are not retired yet, so you still need to prove yourselves skilled enough to be reporters on the *Sedalia Star* payroll, understand?"

"Yes, sir!" we said in unison.

But before Mr. Jacobs could give our next assignments, the phone sitting on his desk rang.

"Hello?" he answered.

Since we couldn't understand the person on the phone, the conversation was mostly one-sided.

"Yes, this is the *Sedalia Star*. What? What is he doing? All right, thanks a lot!"

"What was that about, boss?" asked Joe. "Who was on the phone?"

"First off, don't call me boss, Vantrice!" said Mr. Jacobs. "And second, that lunatic scientist Dr. Kingston is at it again!"

"What do you mean, sir?" Rachel asked.

"That was his son, Bobby, on the phone. He's somehow managed to give himself explosive superpowers!" Mr. Jacobs replied. "Well, what are you waiting for? Get on this story, but stay safe! Now!"

"Yes, sir!" we said all together.

As we began to head out of the office and into the hallway, Annie pulled me aside.

"Hey, Leon?" she asked.

"Yes?" I replied.

"Before you go call your dad again," she said, "I want you to know that I'm sorry that we got into that fight earlier."

"I'm sorry too," I said. "Do you want to call it even?"

She grabbed me, and we both leaned into a hug, reconciling our friendship.

"Please be careful out there, Leon," she said as we gazed into each other's eyes.

"I will, Annie," I replied.

As we turned and went our separate ways, I ran into the nearest rooftop access and changed into my Leoman costume. Afterward, I climbed down the side of the building, then confronted the formally good doctor downtown near city hall. The city streets were being evacuated because of Dr. Kingston's explosive rampage. As he continued to project his orange colored electrical energy blasts in a circular radius around himself, he was causing nearby cars to explode and nearby buildings to catch on fire.

"Hold it right there, Dr. Kingston!" I said with a roar.

"Dr. Kingston?" he shouted. "That name doesn't even begin to describe my power!"

He fired another of his explosive energy blasts, this time aiming at me. Thankfully, I dodged it unscathed using my lion-like agility and reflexes.

"I now possess the power of an explosive!" he shouted. "No, I *am* an explosive!"

As he kept firing more energy blasts, which felt like hot steam even though I kept dodging them, I realized that maybe I could try knocking him out with the tranquilizer gun that I had used to defeat the Human

Hydra. Joe had started calling it the Crime Tamer ever since, to my annoyance.

Okay, then, I thought. *Let's try this and see what happens.*

That's when I grabbed the Crime Tamer, loaded some of the light blue tranquilizer darts filled with the anti-FANG formula my mom created and tried to shoot some at him. But he fired his energy wave and vaporized them before they could reach their target. I hid behind an abandoned car to figure out my next move to stop him for good.

Oh, great, I thought. *Now how am I supposed to stop this guy?*

I heard a sharp beep coming from my right ear.

"Leon, Leon!" shouted my mom. "Are you there, bud?"

"Mom?" I shouted back. "Since when do I have a radio in my mask?"

"Did you think the Crime Tamer was the only upgrade to your Leo-Suit?" asked Joe.

"We'll talk about this later, Joe," I said sternly. "Now, how do I stop this C4 guy?"

"Did you try using the Crime Tamer?" asked Joe.

"Yes, I did," I said. "The tranquilizer darts didn't work on him."

"Well, did you try getting closer?" asked my mom.

"I'm trying to, Mom," I replied, "but every time I try getting close enough to hit him, he projects another energy blast at me."

"Well, then," said Joe, "try taking him down with a new, stealthier approach."

"What do you mean, Joe?" I asked.

"It's time for another one of your suit's new upgrades," explained Joe, "something that your mom did with the tranquilizer formula in some of your darts."

"Say what?" I exclaimed.

"Do you see the darts with the dark violet casing on them?" my mom asked.

"Yes, ma'am," I said after I found them in one of the pouches on my belt. "Now what do I do?"

"Take a step back, then throw one on the ground," my mom explained. "The forceful impact should do the rest."

"Should?" I asked, a little more than concerned.

"Just do it before he tries to blast you again!" shouted Joe.

I threw the dart on the ground and instantly a huge cloud of violet smoke sprayed out of the dart, blinding Dr. Kingston in the process.

"You guys are a pair of mad geniuses!" I exclaimed.

As I snuck up behind him through the smoke while he was standing in the middle of the street, I tried to pounce on him like a lion while using my lion-like night vision. Dr. Kingston's anger finally reached its peak.

"Enough!" he screamed.

As he did, he fired one last energy wave that was larger and more powerful than before, which blasted in all directions. The shockwave of the energy wave sent me flying mid-pounce into the side of a nearby building. When I slammed into the building, part of the wall fell on top of me, knocking me out.

Just before Dr. Kingston tried to finish me off for good, a familiar evil voice spoke into his mind through thought.

Wait! Mind-Breaker commanded sternly. *He's no one!*

"Who dares to command a man with the power of a C4 explosive?" shouted Dr. Kingston.

The man who gave you the means to become who you are.

"What do you mean?" Dr. Kingston exclaimed.

All will be made clear in time, he said calmly. *For now, call me Mind-Breaker.*

"What do you want, Mind-Breaker?" Dr. Kingston demanded.

To help you get revenge, he said smiling. *But first, we need to find a better way for you to channel your new gift.*

The next thing I knew, Dr. Kingston was gone, and I was waking up half an hour later to Joe yelling at me in my face.

"Leon, are you there?" he yelled. "Leon!"

"All right, all right, Joe," I groaned. "I'm here. What's up?"

"Oh, man." Joe signed with relief. "I thought I'd never hear that voice of yours again."

"You and me both, bud," I said, brushing the dust and rocks out of my costume.

"Leon, are you okay?" my mom asked.

"Yes, I'm fine, Mom," I reassured her.

I suddenly remembered what had happened.

"Wait, where's Dr. Kingston?" I asked, worried.

"We don't know, son," my mom said. "But …"

"But what, Mom?" I asked, concerned.

"He broke into the mayor's office and took him hostage," she said.

"So what are we going to do, Leon?" asked Joe.

"Well, I think I might have an idea on how to save the mayor," I said as I thought of a plan. "But first, Joe, I need to know exactly what kind of upgrades you put in my costume."

"It's called a Leo-Suit!" Joe quickly objected.

"Of course it is, Joe," I replied sarcastically.

As I was making my way back to Mom's lab, my dad was hard at work at the Sedalia City Police Department. After going over what seemed like hours of evidence, trying to find something he may have overlooked on the Kingston case, one of his police lieutenants, Shawn Richards, came rushing into his office.

"Captain Garrett, Captain Garrett!" he called out, almost crashing into the glass door.

"Yes, yes, what is it, Richards?" Dad asked.

"We've got an anonymous tip saying that Dr. Kingston was spotted heading into the Baker Chemical Plant," he said as he was catching his breath.

"Are we absolutely sure it's him?" Dad asked.

"Yes, sir," he replied, handing my dad a photograph. "We just got this off one of the security cameras on site, and we ran it through the facial recognition software."

"Get a SWAT team ready," Dad said. "I want this madman locked up before dawn!"

"Yes, sir," he said while leaving my dad's office.

"Make sure the media warns the public to call us for more sightings," Dad said. "Give them his description!"

While Dad was trying to get a SWAT team together, Joe's voice came over the radio in my mask again.

"Hey, Leon," he said, "are you there?"

"Yes, I am," I replied. "What's up?"

"Sid just texted me," he said. "He's arranged an interview with Dr. Kingston's son."

"Where and when?" I asked.

"On the rooftop of the Children's Library on the corner of Second Street and Dawn Avenue in one hour," he replied.

"Okay, then," I said. "Let me find somewhere to change into my normal clothes, and I'll be there as fast as I can."

The sun had finished setting on the city after I found a nearby alleyway and got changed. Since I was on a time crunch, I checked my surroundings before leaping up to the rooftop. Just as I landed, I saw a frazzled-looking Bobby finish drinking something out of a test tube.

"Excuse me," I said. "Are you Bobby Woods?"

"Who are you?" he asked. "What do you want?"

"My name is Leon Garrett," I replied politely. "My friend Sid said you might know where your father is."

"What?" he asked. "Why, did he send you?"

"No, he didn't," I replied, "but the police are looking for him, and any information you can give might be beneficial."

"You can't stop him," he said, shuddering. "Nothing can stop him!

But with this antigravity serum, yes, with this, I can go to Neverland, where he can never hurt me again!"

"Neverland?" I asked. "You know that's only a fairy tale, right?"

"No, it's not! It's real! I'll show you! I'll show you all!"

"I'm sorry. Maybe we should get you to a doctor."

"No!" he screamed. "I'm going to Neverland, and there's no one who's going to stop me!"

He popped the cork off the test tube in his hand and drank all the contents from it before I could stop him. As if by magic and defying the natural laws of physics, he started floating in midair, and then, with an almost wicked glee, he flew around the rooftop before my very eyes.

"Now, do you believe, Mr. Garrett?" He laughed. "Well, do you?"

When he was flying around the edge of the rooftop, his serum began wearing off, and he started falling to the ground. I managed to grab onto his hand just before he plummeted toward the sidewalk below.

"Hang on!" I said. "Don't worry. Everything's going to be fine."

With barely any effort, thanks to my lion strength, I pulled him back up to the rooftop unharmed.

"You could've killed yourself!" I shouted. "What were you thinking?"

"What does that matter," he said passively. "I flew!"

"You really don't care whether you live or die?" I shouted as I grabbed ahold of him and looked him in the eyes.

"But I flew," he said to me in an almost childlike voice.

When I finally realized it was just a waste of time talking to him, I figured I couldn't just leave him after what he just did. I dropped him off at the front entrance of Sedalia General Hospital and decided it was time to meet up with Joe at my mom's lab.

After a half, an hour I walked into the lab building. A few minutes after I got to Mom's lab at the Sedalia City Zoo, Joe quickly grabbed me and started yanking down the long narrow hallway to her office.

"Come on, Leon!" he said with a panicked look on his face.

"What's going on, Joe?" I asked as I easily wrested from his grip.

"Just come on, man!" he said.

We began running down to my mom's office, where she was sitting in her desk chair watching the news while holding back the tears in her eyes.

"Mom, what's wrong?" I asked.

"It's all over the news! Your father's been taken hostage!" she shouted. "Now that monster's demanding one million dollars in exchange for both Mayor Early's and your father's life!"

"What about the mayor?" I asked.

"We're thinking that he's got other plans for him, Leon," Joe replied.

"Joe, you've got to tell me all the upgrades you put into the Leo-Suit, now!" I demanded.

"All right, bud," Began Joe. "Your suit is made of a thin layer of Kevlar and Nomex, making it bullet and temperature resistant. Your mask has a radio that doubles as a police scanner, and your darts have different types for different purposes like explosives, electrical shock, as well as the smoke screen one that you used earlier."

"Is there anything else?" I asked.

"Nope, that's pretty much it," he replied.

"Good," I said. "Then I'm out of here."

"Wait, what?" asked Joe as he grabbed my arm. "Where are you going?

"I'm going to go save my dad and the mayor!" I replied, freeing myself from his grip and rushing off on my mission. Since I didn't know where they were, I used my lion-like sense of smell to track down Dr. Kingston by his scent. When I finally got his scent a few minutes later, I started to track him down.

"Good luck," he said under his breath.

While I was busy trying to track down Dr. Kingston's scent, he was hiding out in the plant manager's office at Baker Chemical. He was testing to see how well he was fitting in the new bulky metal containment suit, which was painted black and orange, when his new benefactor appeared from out of nowhere.

"Are we enjoying our new gift, my friend?" Mind-Breaker said, smirking.

"Maybe I would enjoy this more if I knew what price I have to pay for it," said Dr. Kingston as he looked himself over thoroughly at the black and orange spandex-like suit, which had been built as a method to contain the excess energy in his body without harm to himself.

"We can worry about that later," he said passively.

"Really?" Dr. Kingston asked sarcastically.

"It's not your concern," he said, annoyed. "Now, get ready. We have guests arriving soon."

"What about this Leoman person who attacked me earlier?" Dr. Kingston asked.

"Don't worry about him," he said with an evil smile. "I've got something planned for that so-called hero."

By the time I could finally track Dr. Kingston to the Baker Chemical plant using my lion-like senses, the police were already on their way there. I decided to follow them, but if I was going to save my dad and the mayor, I would have to sneak in and find a hiding spot quickly before they did the exchange. So, moving with the speed, grace, and dexterity of a jungle cat, I leapt from the side of a nearby building, swung off a tree branch, and finally landed through an open window onto the floor of the corner office of the top right side of the building. I snuck down through the hallways as I searched the offices for the mayor using my lion-like senses.

When I got down to the front door of the foreman's office above the shipping dock, I heard the commotion of the SCPD coming through the shipping dock entrance. As I listened in on the conversation between them and C4 who was waiting for them, I realized they might be able to keep him busy with the hostage/ransom exchange long enough for me to break the lock off the office door quietly and check to see if Mayor Early was being held up inside.

"Did you bring the money?" C4 asked the police officers.

"Yes, we did, Dr. Kingston," said one of them.

"My name is C4 now," he said with an annoyed tone. "Now, give me the money."

"Give us Captain Garrett and the mayor first," said another.

"Do you want them with or without heads?" he said as he started to get angry. "Give. Me. My. Money. Now!"

"All right, C4," said the first officer.

I watched as he sat a bulletproof briefcase down on the ground at C4's feet.

"You have your money. Now give us Captain Garrett and the mayor," he demanded.

"Very well," said C4 very casually. "You can have Captain Garrett back."

When he went to go get my dad, I felt a wave of sorrow and guilt wash over me as I thought it was my fault he was in serious danger. Or at least, a good part of it was my fault because I couldn't defeat C4 in the first place.

A few minutes later, he came back with my dad. His hands behind his back in a pair of handcuffs. He walked silently past C4 to the awaiting group of police officers.

"Wait," said the second police officer again. "What about the mayor?"

"What about him?" asked C4 impatiently. "The one million dollars was for Captain Garrett, not for the mayor. Now get out."

"Hey, wait a minute," protested the police officer.

C4 then projected an energy blast at the police officers, nearly getting some of their heads blown off by the energy blast.

"I said get out!" C4 shouted, enraged.

The police officers made a quick and hasty retreat with my dad alongside them.

Seeing that my dad was safe from the hallway on the upper deck, I finally took the chance and broke the lock along with the doorknob with a quick flick of my wrist. Once I got inside the foreman's office, I spotted the mayor tied up in a chair on the other side of the front office.

"Don't worry, Mayor Early," I said. "I'll get you out of here."

"No, don't!" he shouted. "It's a trap!"

A series of sharp electronic beeps started screeching in my ears. Just my luck. I was so focused on saving the mayor that I didn't notice the speakers in the room. Mind-Breaker and C4 came out of hiding from the back office. They just stood there in front of me, gloating about how I carelessly fell into their trap. Unbeknownst to them both, I managed to barely overhear their conversation thanks to Joe teaching me to resist certain sounds after the hair-salon incident.

"Brilliant play, Mind-Breaker," said C4. "Please, tell me again how this is possible?"

"Well as you can see, C4," Mind-Breaker began, "the speakers are emitting a high-frequency pulse. Think of it as a giant dog whistle. We can't hear it, but I suspected that he might since he was able to track us here so quickly."

"I still say it's very clever, Mind-Breaker," said C4. "Now, when do I get my revenge?"

"Do not speak to me like that again!" Mind-Breaker started choking C4 with his telekinesis. "Because the last person who did got his mind crushed!"

"Okay … okay … I got it!" C4 said, gasping.

"Great!" he said cheerfully as he released his telekinetic grip. "Now I have other things I need to attend to. I trust you can finish our would-be hero before melting the mayor's head into a puddle?"

"Yes," said C4, holding his enraged tongue. "You can trust me."

Despite being able to hear them, however, the speakers were loud and painful to my ears. However, I thought of an idea. If I could resist the frequency long enough to use my lion strength and claws to tear apart the speakers, it would stop. So, using my lion strength, I leapt over to the first one nearest to me and used my retractable claws to slice it into large pieces. I sent each of the pieces hurtling toward the others, which destroyed them. The pair of villains stopped laughing and paired to fight me.

"Looks like it's time for you to face the music, C4!" I shouted.

"In your dreams, you wannabe hero!"

He blasted at me. Thankfully, I dodged the blasts with my leonine speed, reflexes, and agility. As he tried to hit me, I finally got close enough to try to knock him out with one blow. Unfortunately, when I did, try it only staggered him and made him even more angry.

"Is that your best shot?" He laughed. "Here, try one of mine!"

That's when he blasted me with so much force, I was sent flying through a nearby wall and fell all the way down from the twelve-story building, crashing into the pavement below. As C4 came down using his energy blasts to safely slow his descent, I staggered to my feet thanks to my healing abilities helping me to survive the fall.

"You're not getting away with this, C4!" I shouted.

"You think you can stop me now, little man? No one can stop me!"

That's when I noticed that as he was charging up to finish me off, his body was sparking with electricity, just like his K-Bomb that I had crushed. I got an idea. All I needed was some water. Luckily for me, I managed to land near a fire hydrant. Moving quickly, I used my animal strength to knock the top off the fire hydrant with a single kick, then used my foot to aim the gushing water at C4, spraying him with it and literally giving him the shock of his life. He fell to the ground, unconscious. Before I left the scene, I climbed my way back up to the office, freed the mayor, and made sure the police found him and arrested C4. Unfortunately, it looked as if Mind-Breaker had vanished once again.

A few days after C4's arrest, I was still feeling confused about how Annie and I had almost kissed at the dance. I mean, did I want a relationship at the time, yes. But would I also be lying to her a lot, yes.

Because she would want to know where I was and what I was doing at the time. What would I even say? Oh, yes Annie, I'm just going around the city in a lion costume, beating up bad guys with superpowers! I wouldn't be surprised if she'd laughed it off or ran away and fear me for the rest of her life. Plus, what if I did tell her about Leoman or worse, my enemies found out who I was and tried to harm her because of me? Then my phone buzzed in my pocket. It was Annie. Crud! She wanted to meet me at the front of the school! What was I going to do? With a heavy sigh, I decided to man up and meet her there.

When I got to the school, she was standing next to the flagpole waiting with a sad look on her tear-stained face with her arms folded across her chest. This wasn't going to end well at all.

"Hi Leon, we need to talk." She sighed.

I could tell from the look on her face she'd been crying long before I got there. This definitely wasn't going to end well.

"Of course, Annie," I replied. "What's wrong?"

"Remember at the dance, how you almost kissed me?" she asked. "It was really flattering to know you feel that way about me."

In all honesty, it made me slightly happy she remembered. But of course, this wasn't the right time to smile, so I kept it to myself.

"How could I forget?" I said. "It was one of the best moments in my life."

"Well, I don't know if I'm ready for a relationship yet," she said. "I appreciate our friendship as it is, and I don't want to lose that."

"Oh, Annie. You could never lose me as a friend," I exclaimed, "but do you think you'll be ready for a relationship with me someday?"

"I do have feelings for you," she replied, "but I don't know if I can be in a relationship with someone who keeps secrets from me."

"I have feelings for you too," I said, "but the secrets I keep are for your protection."

"I have to completely trust you, but I'm no damsel in distress."

"I never said you were. You're a strong, independent young woman."

"Then just be honest with me," she begged. "I can take whatever secrets you have."

I wanted to tell her so badly, but I made a promise to my parents that I wouldn't tell anyone. Besides, if she knew the truth about me, I figured she'd either scoff in my face, thinking I was just being a jerk, or she'd run away from me in fear and never want to speak to me again. So I decided not to tell her—for her sake as well as mine.

"I want to tell you so badly," I said, "but I can't."

"You can't or you won't?"

"I'm sorry, Annie, but it's both."

"I feel like I don't know you anymore," she said with a tear running down her face.

"I'm still the same guy you met at church over a year ago. I'm just private about some things, but my intention is to never hurt you. I hope we can still be friends."

"I can respect that. After all, we will always be friends, but I need some space to think."

"Okay. Call me when you're ready to talk."

"See you around, Leon," she said sadly.

"See you around, Annie."

I sighed as she walked away. The sad mood was broken with my phone buzzing in my pocket. Joe was calling me.

"Hey, Joe." I sighed. "What's up?"

"Hey, Leon. Where are you?"

"I'm at school. Why?"

"Are you alone?" he asked.

"I am now. What's going on?"

"Good, because Bobby Woods just escaped from the psych ward of Sedalia General Hospital."

"What? Don't tell me—he flew out the window, right?"

"Yes!" he exclaimed. "But how'd you know?"

CHAPTER 6
WHO IS THE MODERN PETER PAN?

While I was on my way to the hospital, there was another visit to at the county jail this time for the now powerless Dr. Kingston, who was waiting in a jail cell pending his trail.

"Well, hello Dr. Kingston," Mind-Breaker said.

"Mind-Breaker! What are you doing here?"

"I've come to kick a dog while he's down," Mind-Breaker said sternly. "Especially since that dog has failed me!"

"It's not my fault! If I wasn't weighted down by distractions from my idiot son, I could've perfected my K-Bomb fuel and destroyed that Leoman guy!"

"Well, he may be delusional, but he may still be of use to my plans."

"What?" he shouted.

"At least I'll be dealing with a better man," Mind-Breaker said as a farewell to his former associate.

"No! *No*!" he screamed. "That fool is worthless! I'm the better man! Mind-Breaker? Mind-Breaker! I'm the better man! I'm the better man!"

A few hours after talking to Annie, I rushed over to the hospital to meet Joe, so we could investigate Bobby's room. Joe was waiting outside an open door of the main entrance.

"Leon, where the heck have you been, man?"

"Sorry, Joe," I said.

Joe noticed the depressed look on my face.

"What's with the long face, buddy?"

"Oh, it's Annie. She doesn't trust me anymore."

"Oh, I'm really sorry Leon."

"It's okay, Joe. Maybe working on this case will help clear my head."

"Good idea. Let's see if we can get one of the doctors or nurses to show us where Bobby was staying."

"Excuse me, miss?" Joe asked a nurse as she passed by us.

"Yes, how may I help you boys?"

"My name is Leon Garrett. This is my partner, Joe Vantrice. We're from the *Sedalia Star.*"

"We're here about Bobby Woods," Joe said, "the young man who supposedly flew out of your psych ward?"

"Why, yes, of course. Our psych ward is right this way, gentlemen."

As she led us to the psych ward, we began asking her details about the incident.

"It must've been quite the peculiar case," I said.

"Yes, it was! One minute, he was strapped to the bed. The next, he's busting out a window and flying out it like a human-sized bird!"

"Was there anything he could've used to make his escape?" Joe asked.

"Well, we found two items by his bed—an empty vial with a greenish-yellow liquid and an empty spray can that was stolen from one of the cleaning staff."

"Wait!" I exclaimed. "Did you say an empty vial?"

"Why, yes."

"Oh, crud!" I exclaimed, running out of the room.

"What?" Joe asked. "What are you—hey, Leon! Wait!"

"There's no time, Joe!"

"No time?" Joe asked, stopping me in my tracks. "What in the world are you talking about, Leon?"

"Look, Joe! When I met up with Bobby for our interview, he was testing an antigravity formula on himself, which nearly got him killed in the process!"

"Wait! So that means—"

"That's right, Joe. If the formula failed him before, who's to say it won't fail again?"

"Looks like we're going to need Leoman," Joe said quietly.

"For once, I agree with you. I'm going to go get changed."

"Wait!" Joe called out as I ran for the nearest bathroom. "What do you want me to do?"

"Stay on the communications and let me know if you find anything!"

"You got it, buddy," Joe said. "Now, go get him, Leoman."

After I changed into my Leoman costume, I spent a couple of hours of searching the entire city from the rooftops, as nighttime had begun to set in on the entire city. I was standing on the rooftop of an apartment complex when my phone started buzzing. It was my dad.

"Hey, Dad, are there any leads from the police?"

"No, not yet Leon. However, there was a missing person's report that just passed my desk about twenty minutes ago."

"Who is it, Dad?"

"A teenage girl by the name of Ariel Swanson. She went missing a short time ago. We already have some officers on sight, but they're not turning up any leads at all."

"Uh, Dad. I think that I found her."

"What, what do you mean?"

"I mean I literally see her hanging on to someone, someone who's actually flying through the air!"

"Wait, what? Someone flying? How's that possible?"

"I don't know how, Dad, but all I know is she's in danger and I need to save her now!"

"All right, son. Please be careful."

"Don't worry, I will. I'm sorry, Dad. I've got to go now!"

"Good luck, Leon!" he said before I hung up on him.

There was no time to waste. I had to do something before his formula failed him again or worse and he got them both killed. So, without hesitating, I ran to the edge of the rooftop, leapt into the air, and managed to land on his back while they were passing by me in midair.

"Hey!" he exclaimed with a familiar voice. "What are you doing?"

"Bobby?"

"No! I'm not Bobby. I'm Elfwood, the modern-day Peter Pan!"

"Elfwood. Have you gone crazy? There's no such thing as Peter Pan!"

"Yes, there is!" he screamed. "I'm the new Peter Pan!"

That's when he started to try and shake me off him while I was trying to frantically punch and kick him to knock him out and save Ariel. Eventually, I managed to climb up, move my hands up to his face, and cover his eyes to block his eyesight. Unfortunately, it didn't go quite exactly as planned, because I accidently forced the three of us to crash into a brick wall off the side of an old building. This made Bobby release his grip on Ariel and, causing her to plummet toward the pavement. Thankfully, I saved her by clinging my claws onto the side of the building to slow and finally stopping our descent.

"All right," I panted. "Are you okay?"

"Yes! Yes, I'm fine!" she said. "I just want to go home!"

"Don't worry," I said. "I'll get you home. I promise."

Bobby swooped down from out of nowhere and grabbed her right out of my hand and started flying away.

"Help. Help me, please!"

"Don't worry, my new friend!" Bobby shouted. "We're on our way to Neverland! That red lion guy will never be able to find us there!"

I tried my best to follow them from the rooftops, but Bobby was going too fast for me to catch up and was pulling farther and farther away from me with each second. Sadly, there was nothing I could do. I was literally forced to watch them get away. I felt so bad about the situation, I considered it one of the worst mistakes I made in my early years as a superhero. It was one of my worst confidence breaker moments in my life. My phone buzzed, again. It was Dad. *Oh, boy.*

"Uh, hey, Dad!" I said nervously. "What's up?"

"Meet me at the police station, as Leon, *now*!"

As I would find out in a few minutes, after I changed back into my regular clothes and got inside the police station, the worst was yet to come. When I stepped inside my dad's office, I noticed Joe was sitting in a chair facing his desk. The chair next to it, however, was meant for me.

"Hey, wait a minute, Dad. What's Joe doing here?"

"Sit down!"

"Yes, sir."

"Now, what happened out there?" he asked.

That's when I told him about Bobby and the reason I hung up on him. I realized I never should've hung up on my dad.

"How could you let him get away with Ariel? Next time, stay on the phone and let me send some choppers to back you up!"

"Yes, sir," I said quietly.

"Okay, now—" he said before the sound of his phone ringing interrupted him. "This is Captain Garrett. What? Don't worry. We'll do everything we can to get her back safely."

"What's wrong, Dad?"

"Bobby's struck again. He's kidnapped Annie right from her bedroom window!"

"What? What are we waiting for? We've got to save them!"

"Hold on, Leon," Dad said. "We don't even know where she or Ariel are!"

"Don't worry, Dad," I reassured him. "I can track her by the scent of her perfume. Plus, I already have a plan."

"All right, son." Dad sighed. "I trust you. But as soon as you find them, let us know. Do you understand?"

"Yes, sir," I said with a slight smile on my face.

That's when I started running out of Dad's office so I could change into my Leoman costume.

Meanwhile, Elfwood was held up with his two captives in a shipping warehouse at the White River Dockyards, which had been abandoned for several decades. Annie and Ariel, who looked similar, were tied up with ropes and placed side by side on dusty metal floor. Along with their insane captor was the man really pulling the strings of his unwitting puppet.

"I didn't know which one you wanted, Mind-Breaker," Elfwood said with a childlike smile. "So I brought you more than one."

"Well Elfwood, my friend," said Mind-Breaker with a sinister smile, "it looks like you're on your way to getting the location to Neverland."

"Really? Ooh, I can't wait! I can't wait!"

"Now, now, now," Mind-Breaker reminded him. "Don't be so impatient. I still have to scan their minds for my chosen one."

"Oh, yes!" Bobby said. "Yes, Mind-Breaker."

"Now, let's see," Mind-Breaker said as he came close to Ariel's face. "Are you my Maria?"

"Maria?" Ariel asked, confused. "What are you talking about, you creep? I want to go home! Help! Help!"

"Well, don't worry. This'll only take a few minutes."

He placed his hand on top of her forehead and began reading her mind. He was searching her memories as he painfully ripped through them, like someone tearing apart papers, piece after piece. she screamed in agony as she felt her mind being ripped apart, and her ears began to bleed.

"Stop it!" Annie shouted. "Leave her alone!"

"Don't worry, young lady," Mind-Breaker said. "Your turn is coming up next."

I busted through the ceiling and confronted the kidnapping villains. I figured that they didn't realize that I had memorized Annie's favorite perfume by heart and tracked her down thanks to my animal-keen sense of smell.

"Let them go now, you creeps!" I shouted.

"You fool!" Mind-Breaker scolded Bobby. "He must've gotten your scent and tracked you here!"

"Well, how was I supposed to know?" he said, confused.

"Well, if you ever want to see Neverland," Mind-Breaker said angrily. "Get over there and stop him before I finish with these two!"

That's when Bobby took to the skies again within the walls of the warehouse and started slashing at me with a small knife, with every few swings or so, he managed to succeed. The blade tore through the Kevlar and Nomex fibers of my costume with one slash across my upper back and one near my right shoulder. That was the last straw and I decided to go on the offensive.

So I leapt up to the second level of the warehouse and hid myself in the shadows where he couldn't see me. Thankfully, he didn't notice, or cut open, the small backpack sown on my costume. Usually it's where I store big pieces of evidence from crime scenes. But this time, I grabbed a net used for catching monkeys and other small animals from the zoo, before coming to save the hostages. I unfolded it and snuck up behind Bobby while he was still searching for me, grabbed him with the net and punched his head into the ground, knocking him out with one blow.

Just as I won my victory against Bobby, Mind-Breaker started choking me with his telekinetic powers. I felt like the air was leaving my lungs and my limbs were paralyzed as I floated in midair.

"Leoman, I don't know who you are underneath that mask of yours, but I intend to find out before I kill you for interfering with my plans!"

"No, stop!" Annie begged. "Please, stop!"

We felt a huge wave of energy that felt like the tremor from an earthquake. It slammed Mind-Breaker so hard, it knocked him off his feet and freed me from his telekinetic grip.

"Maria?" Mind-Breaker groaned as he stood back up. "My beautiful daughter, is that you?"

That's when I tried and sadly failed to tackle him.

"This isn't over, Leoman!" he shouted as he disappeared without a trace once again into the darkness.

"Dang it! He got away again!"

I heard the approaching police sirens, so I decided to cut Ariel and

Annie loose and make a hasty exit, leaving Bobby in the net and before either one could say a word to me.

Afterward, I left the scene to change back into my street clothes, then ran back to find my dad watching the other police officers taking Bobby away in a stray jacket. Annie and Ariel's parents were at the scene, holding their daughters so tightly, it seemed they would never let go again. I approached my dad to apologize to him for running out of his office.

"Hey, Dad—"

"It's okay, Leon. You did a good job here tonight. I'm proud of you."

"Thanks, Dad," I said, thankful he wasn't mad at me.

As we all made our way home, Mind-Breaker decided to visit another failure in No Man's Land Penitentiary. This time, it was in their intensive psychiatric ward.

"Is this Neverland?" Bobby asked while in a confused state from all the medication in his body.

"No," he said in a stern tone.

He pulled out a cell phone and dialed an unknown number on speed dial.

"I am willing to pay you with any means and any price," he said to a mysterious person on the phone. "Send this message to the best mercenary or assassin you can possibly think of!"

"Well, what's the job, sir?" the person said.

"I want Leoman *dead*!" he shouted.

"Oh, sure, sure, sir!" the person said cunningly, "but, uh, why do you want this Leoman guy dead so badly?"

"Because it seems like he's the only one with the power to stop my plans. Now, will you put the word out or not?"

"But of course, sir," the person said with a chuckle. "Of course we will."

CHAPTER 7
HOW FAR DOES THE SILVER STAR FALL?

A few weeks after C4 and Elfwood were defeated and Mind-Breaker disappeared yet again from the scene of the crime without a trace, Joe and I got a call from Mr. Jacobs in the afternoon after school had let out for the day. He wanted us to meet him at his office for our next assignment. When we got there, it seemed as if all the other reporters were clocking out for the day as well while we began ours. As we came up and knocked on the door to his office.

"Yeah, who is it?" he shouted.

"It's Leon and Joe, sir."

"Who?" he asked, not realizing it was us.

"It's Garrett and Vantrice, boss," Joe said. "You called us for an assignment?"

"Stop calling me boss, Vantrice! Now, get in here!"

"Yes, Mr. Jacobs," I replied as we entered his office.

"Sit down, boys," he said as he opened a cigar case and lit one. This was a rare thing he did at the office, which usually meant he was under a lot of stress about giving us a new assignment.

"Are you all right, sir?" I asked.

"Fine, Garrett. I'm fine," he said, grumbling almost to himself.

"Now listen up, you two. Have either one of you heard of the Triple W tournaments?"

"You mean the World Wrestling Wars tournaments?" asked Joe sarcastically. "Yeah, who hasn't?"

"I haven't," I said, somewhat embarrassed.

They both gave me a look saying, *What is wrong with you?*

"What?" I exclaimed. "My parents don't allow me to watch wrestling or stuff like that at all!"

"Remind me to help you with that later, Leon," Joe said with a smirk.

"Can it, you two? Now, this month, the finals of the Triple W tournament are going to be at the Luigi Stadium building here in Sedalia City. Since all of my top reporters have the day off tomorrow, I want you two at the tournament tomorrow night covering the events for our Sunday special. Got that?"

"Yes, sir!" we said in unison.

"Then what are you two still doing here? Move it! Get ready for that tournament tomorrow night!"

"Well, looks like our weekend plans are cancelled," I said sarcastically as we hurried out of Mr. Jacobs's office.

"Huh?" Joe remarked. "Sarcasm. Looks like your social skills are improving."

"Ha, ha, ha," I said with a sarcastic chuckle. "Very funny, Joe. Very funny."

The night of the Triple W tournament came, and the stadium parking lot was packed full of the vehicles. It seemed as if the whole city was there. There were even security guards at the gates to keep people from getting in after the ticket stands sold out for the event. Thankfully, our press badges were enough to gain us entry, and we got in the parking lot. As we walked into the stadium, I stopped Joe.

"What's up, Leon?"

"I'm not sure if I can do this story, Joe," I said nervously.

"Really?" he asked, concerned. "Why? What's wrong, Leon?"

"It's just," I explained, somewhat embarrassed. "I don't like it when innocent people fight each other."

"Look, Leon," Joe explained as he pulled me aside from the crowd. "These wrestling tournaments may look brutal, but it's all for show."

"You sure about this, Joe?"

"Of course I am, Leon," he reassured me. "Besides, if something happens in there, you know I got your back, right bud?"

"Yes, Joe," I said, taking a deep breath. "I know you've got my back, and I have yours."

"All right, then." He smiled. "Let's go in and have fun covering this story!"

As we walked in, there was a large square wrestling ring in the middle of the stadium, surrounded by smaller blue rectangular foam mats down the length of both sides of the football field. The stadium seats were packed with fans left and right. After the first two hours of covering most of the tournament's semifinal matches from the press section near the wrestling ring, the last of the women's matches was about to begin.

"Man, Joe!" I finally said as I saw yet another wrestler getting pinned by his opponent. "You said these tournaments were brutal, but this is ridiculous!"

"Are you kidding me now, Leon? That was just the opening act! Now the real fights are about to begin!"

"Really? Good grief! No wonder my parents didn't allow me to watch wrestling!"

"Don't worry, Leon. All these wrestlers are trained athletes."

"Yeah, so what?" I asked sarcastically.

"So that means they're trained to fight, and they get paid to fight."

"Oh, okay," I said, finally understanding. "I'm sorry, Joe."

"It's okay, Leon." He chuckled. "There's no need to apologize. We're cool."

"Thanks, man."

"Hey, look!" Joe said excitedly as the spotlights shone on the ring.

The announcer was wearing a black tuxedo and shiny black shoes with a white button-up shirt, red bow tie, and black sunglasses. He was standing in the middle of the ring, carrying a microphone with a long black cord that extended past the length of the ring and connected all the way back to announcers' table.

"Ladies and gentlemen! Welcome to the last of the ladies' semi-finals! In this corner, weighing in at two hundred and ten pounds, she's the reigning women's world wrestling champion, Sedalia City's own shining Silver Star, Shelley Starr!"

The audience erupted in cheers and applause.

"And in this corner, weighing in at one hundred and ninety-five pounds! Who's crazy enough to try and take the Silver Star's title? The Triple W's own crazy comedic clown, the Jester!"

A referee walked to the center of the ring, between the two fighters.

"All right, ladies, I want a good, clean fight. Are we clear?"

They both nodded in agreement.

"All right, go to your corners and wait for the bell. Here we go! Ready? And … fight!"

Mere seconds after he said the word "fight," the sound of the bell's sharp *clang clang* rang throughout the stadium, and the clash of the female titans begin!

Jester started throwing rapid-fire punches into Shelley's torso. But Shelley countered with a back-handed slap. As Jester stepped backward, recovering from the blow, she startled Shelley by childishly sticking her tongue out at her and wiggling her hands. Enraged, Shelley tried to ram into her in a spearing motion, but Jester leapt into the air and, with her legs in a midair split, evaded Shelley's charge and into one of the corners of the ring. Jester put her hand over her face, laughing as she faced the audience, congratulating herself.

Shelley finally had enough of Jester's clowning around. As both the fighters stood back up and faced each other, Jester tried to throw a haymaker punch at her. As she charged at her, Shelley kicked her knee so hard, it shattered her kneecap. While Jester was screaming with pain, Shelley punched Jester with enough force to break her jaw and make her head hit the mat. As she tried to sit back up, Shelley grabbed her wrapped her left arm around her in a full nelson, forcing her to tap out of the match before passing out from the pain.

As the sound of the bell's sharp *clang clang clang* rang out in the stadium once again, the ringside medics came rushing in to tend to Jester.

"Ladies and gentlemen, tonight's winner and still reigning women's world wrestling champion, Shelley Starr!"

As she was celebrating her victory with the audience cheering for her, something strange started to happen. I couldn't figure out how, but for some odd reason, I smelled a faint odor of a gorilla. But that was impossible since we were nowhere near the Sedalia City Zoo.

"Hey, Joe, do you smell something weird?"

"No, I don't, Leon. Why do you ask?"

"Nothing. I was just wondering," I said, thinking I should keep it to myself until I figured out what was going on with me. When I got some time to step away from the action, I decided to call my mom to see what she thought was happening.

"Hello?"

"Hey, Mom. Are you somewhere private right now?"

"I can be in a few minutes. Why, what's wrong? Are you okay?"

I told her what had happened earlier that evening and about the odor.

"Hmm, that is strange. Would you be okay if we ran some tests at the lab after church tomorrow?"

"Yes, ma'am, as long as there are no needles involved."

"Well, bud, I can't make any promises about that."

As I talked with mom on the phone, I noticed Shelley Starr was walking past me, and I began to smell that same scent of a gorilla. Was it coming from Shelley? I figured there was only one way to find out, so I decided to investigate.

"Hey, Mom, may I call you back? Something's just come up in our news story."

"Okay, Leon. I love you."

"I love you too, mom. Bye."

I decided to start my investigation by following Shelley to her dressing room. Thankfully, I managed to get to there without being seen by her or any backstage security. When I got to her dressing room, the door was barely cracked open. As I got closer to the door, I overheard her talking on a phone to someone thanks to my animal-keen hearing.

"Whatever you gave me, Doc, it really worked," Shelley said.

"So how long did it take to defeat the Jester?" her doctor asked.

"That stupid clown girl? I took her down in less than twenty minutes, but I was faking it the whole time."

"Oh, really? I heard she put up a good fight."

"Listen, Doc," she began to boast just as I secretly started recording what she was saying with my phone. "As long as I got that FANG stuff in me, giving me the strength of a silverback gorilla, I can take on anyone, anytime, anywhere!"

"Good, because that's all I'm giving you."

"What are you talking about? I need that stuff to keep my title!"

"Sorry, but the price has gone up for you keeping that title. You know that drug's been illegal since it turned that Human Hydra thug into a snake monster."

"What do you mean the price has gone up? I've paid you well enough, haven't I? Plus, I'm only taking it in small doses."

"I want double the money, or you can kiss your precious title goodbye the next time you lose."

"All right, fine. You'll get your money!"

As I finished recording their conversation, I heard footsteps approaching me from the other side of the hallway.

"Hey, you!" shouted the security guard. "What are you doing back here?"

"I'm sorry, sir. I'm from the *Sedalia Star*. I was hoping to get an interview with Miss Star."

"The press isn't allowed back here. You'll have to get your story from somewhere else."

He escorted me all the way back to the front gate, where Joe was waiting for me.

"Now, don't let me catch you poking around the dressing rooms again, you understand?"

"Yes, sir," I said as he stormed away.

Joe pulled me aside after we walked back out to the parking lot.

"What were you thinking, Leon? You could've got us into a lot of trouble!"

"Never mind that, Joe!" I said as I pulled out my phone. "Listen!"

I showed him the recording of Shelley Starr and her doctor.

"We have to get this to Mr. Jacobs!" Joe exclaimed as he started up the hippie van.

"We will," I said as we drove away. "But first, we should get this to my dad at SCPD!"

When we got to my dad's office in the Sedalia City Police Department, it looked as if he was on the phone with someone, and by the look on his face, he wasn't happy about it.

"Leon! Joe! Come on in, boys!"

"Yes, sir. What's wrong, Dad?"

"I just got off the phone with the head of security at Luigi Stadium," he said angrily. "Why were you in the dressing room area?"

I told him about the strange smell and handed him the recording I made.

"Well, it looks like I'm going to have to issue Miss Star a search warrant for her residence," my dad said.

"Thank you for understanding, sir."

"Don't you have a story to write for Mr. Jacobs?" he said with a grin.

"Yes, sir. Joe and I are going to get on it right now."

The next day, we were at my mom's lab, testing me to figure out how I had managed to smell the FANG formula in Shelley Star's body. As mom was sticking a needle in me for the umpteenth time to draw a blood sample, we heard on from the newscaster on TV that Shelley Star had been arrested and was in police custody pending her day in court.

"This just in, a local wrestler has been arrested for use of the illegal FANG drug. Because of her actions, the Triple W Tournaments have issued a lifetime ban on her from the competition. She is currently in police custody pending her trail, and a lawsuit is expected from opponent Jessica 'Jester' Jennings for injuries she received during their match."

"Wow!" I exclaimed. "I didn't mean to ruin her career!"

"Well, that's what she gets for taking illegal drugs!" Mom replied. "Now, hold still, son."

"Ow, Mom!" I exclaimed as I felt the needle's painful pinch. "How many more blood tests do you need to run on me?"

"Sorry, Leon. This will be the last one for today."

Joe and my dad came into the lab.

"We came as soon as we could, Dr. Garrett," Joe said.

"How's Leon? Is he all right?"

"I'm fine, Dad. Don't worry, sir," I replied, turning to Joe. "How did Mr. Jacobs react to our story?"

"Oh, believe me, Leon," he said with a smirk, "he's ecstatic!"

"Really? But I ruined Shelley's life. Her career is over because of me."

"Yeah! She was cheating to win!"

"And hurting the other competitors in the process," Dad said. "You did the right thing, Leon. We're all proud of you."

"Thanks, Dad. Now, if you boys are done celebrating," Mom said, "I've got the results of the tests I ran on Leon."

"All right, Amanda," Dad said. "What are they?"

"It appears there are faint traces of the FANG toxin," Mom said, looking at a test tube filled with a blood sample. "You must have inhaled some of it when you fought Human Hydra."

"What?" I exclaimed. "That's impossible! Then why am I not a monster like he was?"

"Apparently, your healing abilities have rendered them harmless to you. They seem to be like dry dead cells in your body."

"Is there any way to get rid of them?"

"Your healing abilities seem to be doing that already, but they also appear to be doing something else."

"Like what, Dr. Garrett?" Joe asked.

"Well, Joe, they appear to have granted Leon a certain level of immunity to the FANG drug as well as an ability to track individuals using it."

"That's great!" Joe exclaimed. "Now Leon's a leonine bloodhound who can track those beastlings!"

"'Beastlings, Joe?" Dad asked. "What are beastlings? What's he talking about?"

"It's just a name he came up with for superhuman FANG users like Human Hydra," I replied, slightly annoyed at Joe. "Don't worry about it, sir."

"Don't worry, Leon. I'm not talking about you," Joe reassured me. "Beastlings are the criminals using that FANG stuff to gain animal-like powers, but the more they use that stuff, the less human they become over time. Using that stuff makes them more and more like the animals whose powers they use."

"He's right, Leon," Mom chimed in. "Your leonine powers came from that lab accident in South Africa. You didn't choose to have powers, but these beastlings, as Joe calls them, become a danger to themselves and those around them. For example, Drac became more and more snakelike as the Human Hydra because he used the FANG drug."

"Well, we have to give these criminals some form of classification, so beastlings it is—at least for now."

"Yes!" Joe said. "I knew you guys would like that name!"

"Yeah, sure Joe," I said sarcastically. "Sure you did, buddy."

Joe's phone and my phone both buzzed in our pockets.

"What is it, Leon?" Mom asked.

"It's Mr. Jacobs," I replied. "He wants to see Joe and me at the newspaper office right now."

"Well, you boys better get a move on," Dad said, "unless your mother doesn't give you a clean bill of health."

"Don't worry, hon, he's good in health."

"All right," Joe said. "Now, come on, Leon. Let's go before your mom changes her mind and runs some more blood tests."

"Good idea," I replied quickly as I ran out the door. "Bye, Mom. Bye, Dad. I'll be home as soon as I can. Love you. Bye."

As I slammed the door behind me, Mom and Dad chuckled. Even though I loved them, I did not want to deal with any more needles for the day.

While Joe and I started heading on our way to the *Sedalia Star*, someone managed to get Shelley Starr out of police custody by posting her fifty-thousand-dollar bail. With her career in ruins because of me, she began trying to plot her next move as she hit a hanging punching bag in her home gym.

"I can't believe that little punk kid ruined me!" she exclaimed to herself. "Somehow, someway, I'll get him back for what he did!"

Unbeknownst to her, a shadowy sinister figure appeared as if from out of nowhere. The figure, knowing full well of the ex-wrestling champion's plight, also knew she had lost all the strength she'd had on the FANG drug and was here with an old familiar power for her to make a deal with him.

"Good evening, Miss Star," greeted Mind-Breaker with an evil smile as he sat casually at her kitchen table without a care in the world. "Or should I just call you Shelley?"

"What?" She gasped in surprise. "Who, what in the world are you?"

"What am I? *What* am I? What a rude thing to ask! Is this how you thank me for bailing you out?"

"How'd you get in here?" she demanded, grabbing her phone. "If you don't leave right now, I'll call the police!"

"No, you won't," he said, snapping his fingers.

She was frozen in place, unable to move her hands to dial and unable to run away in terror.

"Now, I'm here to make you a deal with you. You want the young man who ruined your life dead, and I want his leonine protector dead. I will give you the power to exact your revenge if you kill the both of them for me. So do we have a deal?"

She was unable to answer, as he had just frozen her in place for fun.

"Hmm? What's that? Oh, right. I'm sorry."

He chuckled as he unfroze her with a passive wave of his hand.

"How do you plan to give such a power?" she demanded, panting with fear.

"I'm glad you asked," he said with an evil smile.

He pulled a small glass bottle from his suit jacket that contained a strange liquid glowing a light green.

"What's that supposed to be? More FANG?"

"Why, of course it is, my new associate," he said as began to fill a syringe full of the liquid. "This is a new, more powerful batch of my FANG drug."

"And how's *that* supposed to help me get back at that Leon kid? Last I checked, the FANG drug only gives you powers of animals for a short while?"

"Yes sadly, that is true, but if you fulfill your end of our agreement, I will make sure you never go without a single drop of FANG flowing through your veins again."

"All right, you got a deal, Mr. ...?"

"You can just call me Mind-Breaker," he said as he set the syringe on a nearby table.

"Thanks, Mind-Breaker!"

"And you can thank me after you kill your next two opponents," he said as he disappeared as quickly as he had appeared.

Seizing what she thinks is the opportunity of a lifetime, Shelley Starr injected herself with the FANG drug, beginning her quest for revenge against the young man who ruined her career. And believe me, I was bound to regret it for a long time.

When we got to the *Sedalia Star*, we looked around and saw the lights were turned off and there was no one around to be seen. As we walked toward Mr. Jacobs's office, everything was so dark and quiet, I bet to this day that even without my leonine hearing, I could still hear a pin drop from a nearby desk. Although to be honest, no pins dropped at that time.

"I'm starting to get nervous here, Joe," I said.

"I'm with you there, Leon. Let's get out of here and call your dad."

The lights flipped on, almost blinding us for a second or two. As our eyes adjusted and we prepared for a fight, our friends and coworkers jumped from underneath their desks with excited, happy looks.

“Surprise!” they all shouted.

“H-hey, guys. What’s the occasion?”

“To congratulate you guys on a job well done, of course!” Annie exclaimed.

“Uh-hem!” Mr. Jacobs cleared his throat to get everyone’s attention. “Now that the guests of honor are here, I would like to give them the opportunity of a lifetime. How would you boys like to make your investigative story a more frequent thing?”

“What are you talking about, Mr. Jacobs?” I asked.

“I’m talking about making you and Vantrice official investigative reporters, Garrett!” Mr. Jacobs said with a laugh.

“Are you serious, boss?” Joe said.

“Of course, I’m serious, Vantrice!” he said happily. “And stop calling me boss!”

“Oh, Leon,” Annie said as she gave me a hug, “I’m so happy for you!”

“Thanks, Annie.” I chuckled slightly. “But …”

“But what, Leon? Talk to me.”

“I ruined Shelley’s life,” I said sadly. “Joe told me her career in the Triple W tournaments was her only source of income. Without that—”

“Leon,” Annie said, interrupting me, “she ruined her career and her life when started taking FANG, not to mention she was ruining the lives of other wrestlers by deliberately injuring them.”

“I agree with you. But ”

“But nothing. You did nothing wrong. Just let it go, okay?”

“All right, Annie, I’ll let it go now.”

We heard the sound of a huge explosion coming from the other side of the office, followed by the crashing of glass and screams of terror from some of the party guests. As we recovered from the shock, I looked on in horror at the gigantic, musclebound monster who had once been Shelley Starr! She was more gorilla-like now than human, with massive arms and chest as well as gorilla-like facial features to match her more savage behavior.

"Where is he?" she shouted.

Out of sheer terror, no one said a single word.

"Maybe you puny wimps are hard of hearing! I said where is he?"

"Where's who?" Joe replied sarcastically.

"Where's that loudmouth snitch, Leon Garrett?"

"Sorry, he left the party early," Joe said. "Can someone take a message?"

As Joe distracted her, I snuck away to a nearby closet to change into my Leoman costume. When I finished, I snuck out the window, and using my leonine agility and claws, I climbed around to the other side of the building unseen and through the hole Shelley had made.

"You know, it's really rude to put a big hole in a public building!" I exclaimed, making my presence known.

"Buzz off, Leoman!" Shelley shouted. "I don't have a beef with you!"

"When people start endangering innocent lives, *I* have a beef with them!"

She picked up a large oak desk and threw it at me. I narrowly evaded it.

"First and final warning, hero! Mind your own business, or you'll join that snitch Garrett in the afterlife!"

As our fight ensued, I overheard Joe and Annie starting to evacuate the guests.

"What are you waiting for, Annie?" Joe said. "Let's get out of here! Now while we still can!"

"I'm not leaving without Leon!" she replied.

"Don't worry, Annie! I'm quite sure he's somewhere safe, calling his dad, you know—like he always does."

"I can't believe he abandoned us again! Leon is such a coward!"

"Look, Annie!" Joe said sternly. "Leon may be a lot of things, but he's no coward!"

"Oh, really? Then why isn't he helping us get everyone out of here?"

"Well maybe he's waiting for the police to show up!"

"Or maybe he's cowering underneath a desk somewhere!"

Shelley threw me into a nearby wall, and while I staggered to get back up, Annie and Joe were in the middle of an argument.

"If you guys are done arguing, I could use some help over here!" I said, slightly annoyed.

"Ha! You're gonna need more help than those two wimps!" Silverstar said with an arrogant laugh.

In a fit of rage, I tried to tackle her to the floor, but unfortunately, she was strong enough to stop me in my tracks despite my leonine strength. With a powerful overhead blow, she slammed her superhumanly strong fists into my arms, breaking them like tree branches.

"*Aaahhhh*!" I roared in excruciating pain as I fell onto my knees.

"Humph! So much for the mighty Leoman!" Silverstar chuckled, almost disappointed. "I thought you were going to be more of a challenge!"

With another superhumanly strong blow, she broke my ribs with a single kick. As I started to go into shock from the pain, all I could hear was Silverstar laughing at me. I was broken and defeated, with no way to protect my friends, unable to do anything about the situation at all.

I saw her shove Annie out of the way, grab Joe, and restrain him as if he were a newspaper. As they came back into my line of sight, she glanced at me and laughed as if I were nothing to worry about. She jumped out the giant hole in the wall, taking Joe with her as a hostage.

Not again … not again …

CHAPTER 8
WHO IS GOING TO WIN THE FINAL ROUND?

The next thing I knew, I was waking up in my mom's lab on an examination table. Not again.

"Hey, Mom!" I called out as I sat up. "I'm up and alive, thankfully."

"Hey, bud!" she replied as she came into the lab. "How are your arms and chest feeling?"

"Considering I've got bruises the size of goose eggs instead of broken bones, I think my odds of recovery are improving."

"You should be thankful your father managed to sneak you in here without alerting the security guards."

"You're right. I'm sorry, Mom." I sighed. "Please let me explain what happened."

"Don't worry. I remember what happened between Leoman and Shelley. All that matters now is we save Joe."

"Well, we won't be saving Joe right now." My dad sighed as he walked into the lab. "The commissioner's putting everyone who was involved with the Shelley Star story under police protection, including you. That means if you are spotted outside of our house, you're going to spend a night in a jail cell."

"But, sir! If we're under police protection, who's going to save Joe?"

"I know that, Leon! But the rules are the rules, and even though we don't always agree with them, we still have to follow them. Do you understand?"

"Yes, sir. I understand."

When we got back home late that night, mom and dad sent me to bed because I had school the next day. The police car was parked on the street in front of the house, keeping a watchful eye on our family in case Shelley Starr tried to attack us in the middle of the night. I spent what seemed like hours in my bed thinking—no, worrying—about Joe. I imagined her beating the tar out of one of my closest friends. It was so vivid and painful, I even started to well up with tears in my eyes. My deep anguish was broken when I heard my phone chime. It was a text from Annie saying.

"You need to see this now!"

There was a link to a YouTube video. I clicked on it and was shocked to find Shelley Starr had posted a video.

"Hey, Shelley Star fans!" She smiled aggressively in front of a camera hanging above the ring at Luigi Stadium. "I have a special message for a certain snitch named Leon Garrett! Why don't you come down to Luigi Stadium and take the beating, like a real man! Or your little friend Joey boy's going to take it for you!"

"No, Leon! Stay away from here! She'll kill us both if you," Joe called out as she turned the camera to face him just before the video stopped.

I grabbed my Leoman costume and changed into it. Shelley Starr might have been expecting to beat up Leon Garrett, but she'd be getting a rematch against Leoman instead!

When I got to the stadium, I snuck in and ran onto the field, where I found a large wrestling ring surrounded by TV cameras. Joe was tied up on a corner post and getting beaten up by Shelley Starr.

"Where's your little snitch friend?" she demanded after hitting Joe with the back of her hand for the umpteenth time.

"Forget it, lady!" he exclaimed wearily from the blows he had received. "I'll never rat him out!"

"Then he'll live long enough to see your blood on his hands!" she shouted, raising her hand to hit him one last time.

I made a surprise attack as I roared and tackled her once again, but this time, when she tried to smash my fully healed arms, I evaded her attack with catlike grace and reflexes.

"I don't remember inviting you to this little party, Leoman!"

"Leon Garrett's a friend of mine," I said with a lion-like growl. "So when you mess with his friends, you mess with me!"

"A little late for that!" She chuckled. "Or did you forget I shattered your arms the last time we fought!"

"You're right. But last time, I wasn't using these!"

I unsheathed my claws from within my nailbeds. We charged at each other and clashed head-on, like heavyweight boxers. Every time she took a swing at me, I evaded and slashed at her with my razor-sharp claws. However, even though I inflicted some moderate wounds, it didn't seem to slow her down. As I was about to fall to my knees after eight hours of long fighting and give up out of exhaustion, I saw the Boy in White through my blurry eyes.

"Don't give up, Leon!" he shouted. "Don't give up. You can still beat her!"

"How am I supposed to beat her if I can't even hurt her?" I exclaimed in a daze.

"You must channel your primal instincts to save Joe. Now, take her down!"

Realizing he was right and I had no other option, I dug deep within my heart and felt the flames of righteous fury flow through my veins. As she tried to smash my head, I felt my strength renewed and evaded her blow with moderate ease. I jumped up and kicked her in the chest with both feet into a backflip, which finally stunned her.

"What's the matter, Shelley? Am I a better contender than you thought?"

Shaking off the dazed feeling from my last kick, she got really mad and tried to charge at me. I evaded it by rolling my body over her back with catlike dexterity. She rammed her head into a corner post of the ring, making herself dizzy once again. While she tried to recover, I leapt onto the ropes directly across from her, jumped off them, and slammed my fists on the top of her head, finally knocking her out for the count.

"Wow, Leon!" Joe exclaimed from behind me. "That was one of the best fights I've ever seen!"

After I calmed down, I untied Joe and checked him for any permanent injuries.

"Don't worry, Leon. I'll be fine."

"Good … that's good," I said, panting.

We heard the echoing police sirens approaching the stadium.

"You better go, bud."

"Yeah, right," I said as I hurried and made my escape once again.

After I got home, Annie texted me and told me the masked vigilante Leoman had saved Joe and the police had taken Shelley Star into custody.

The next day at the *Sedalia Star*, Mr. Jacobs called a staff meeting with Joe, Annie, Rachel, and me in attendance.

"All right, everybody! Listen up! Now, for those of you who don't know, that masked vigilante known as Leoman defeated Shelley Starr last night and saved the life of our own intern, Mr. Vantrice. Even though he's taking the law into his own hands, we as a newspaper should be grateful he saved one of our own. However, despite recent events, we need to know who he is and why he's doing this. To that end, I'm assigning Jones and Peters to find and unmask Leoman. Also, I'm assigning my new full-time reporter, Garrett, to follow up on Shelley Starr."

"Please excuse me, sir," I interrupted, "but after what happened to Joe, I don't feel like I'm ready for that kind of responsibly."

"Well …" he said, giving a long thought. "All right, Garrett. You can sit this one out. But the next I say you're ready, you better agree with me, got it?"

"Yes, sir." I sighed with relief. "Thank you for understanding."

"All right, no need to get mushy with me." He chuckled. "Now, get out of here and get some rest. You'll need it for your next assignment."

"You got it, boss." I chuckled as I walked quickly out of his office.

"Quit calling me boss!" he called out.

While I was going home to get some rest, someone else was stewing in his own heated anger. After hearing on the news that another one of his new associates had failed him, Mind-Breaker shut off the TV in frustration. His mood changed slightly when he sensed a cold presence enter his office.

"You're late. Where have you been?"

"I was busy." He smirked. "You don't really think you're my only contract, do you?"

"When I ask to meet with an assassin," Mind-Breaker said, getting angry, "I expect them to show up and get the job done in a timely fashion! Now, do you want the job or not?"

"That depends. When and where would you like me to end your little lion problem?"

CHAPTER 9
WHO IS THE CHILLING HITMAN?

It was a Saturday morning a few weeks after I defeated Shelley Star, around 10:00 a.m. I was sleeping in after another long night of taking down small-time crooks. I was having a vivid nightmare about fighting a man with a light blue knife, as Leoman. He stabbed me through my stomach and killed me. He walked slowly away from my lifeless body, chuckling with an almost wicked glee and a cold-blooded smile on his face.

I woke up to my phone ringing on my bedside table. With a quick wipe of the cold sweat from my forehead and the tears from my eyes, I picked up the phone and answered the call from Joe.

"Hey, Leon. I got some great news!"

"All right, all right, Joe. Slow down. Now, what's the great news?"

"Well, Uncle Roy has been hired by DexTech Industries to transport a top-secret load for them coast to coast, and he wants us to come along and help him out!"

"Wait, what? Please tell me you're kidding, bud."

"No, man. I'm being serious! All we have to do is pick up the load in New York City and take it to Los Angeles."

"Whoa, whoa, wait a minute! That's halfway across the country one way and all the way across the country the other way!"

"Don't worry, Leon. He's getting paid twenty thousand dollars plus expenses, and he's going to split it four ways in exchange for our help!"

"Twenty thousand dollars? Wait—who's the fourth man on this job?"

"Well … Sid's brokering the deal."

"*Say what*?"

I couldn't believe Sid, our resident informant and conman by nature, was going to be the broker of this deal. I had a really horrible feeling about this.

"Yes, he's our middleman," he said.

"Joe, have you lost your mind? For all we know, Sid's setting us up to pay for another one of his scams!"

"Well, for one thing, Leon, I already ran a background check on the entire deal."

"That's reassuring," I said sarcastically, rolling my eyes. "Have you run a background check on Sid recently?"

"And secondly," Joe continued, ignoring my last comment, "despite our criminal past, the Vantrice Family lives by a code, one of the top rules being not to harm the family in any way."

"All right, Joe," I said. "I'll help with this, on one condition."

"What's that, Leon?"

"If Sid does anything stupid, we'll take his share and we'll never work with him again, agreed?"

"I'll agree to that, and I'll do one better," he said. "If he does, I'll let you throw him out of the truck."

"Okay, then. You're on!"

When the day finally came a month later, we met at the DexTech corporate office building in New York City and walked into the main entrance. The lobby was a large and bright with its white walls and light gray tile flooring. Along either side of the lobby were rows of chairs and benches, and toward the back was a large wooden reception desk shaped in a half circle, with four secretaries lined up along the desk, sitting and answering phone calls.

"All right, boys," said Uncle Roy as we came up to the reception desk in his traditional dark red T-shirt and blue jeans. "Let me do the talking, you understand?

"Yes, sir," Joe and I both replied.

"Hello, gentlemen," said the receptionist. "Welcome to DexTech. How may I help you today?"

"I'm Roy Vantrice," said Roy. "We're here to see Mr. Garrett."

"Of course, Mr. Vantrice," she said. "He'll be right with you shortly."

"Wait a minute," I said, shocked. "Did he say, 'Mr. Garrett'?"

"Yes, he did," Joe said. "Why, is everything all right?"

"There's only one Mr. Garrett in our family," I explained. "My older brother, Ryan."

"Your brother? I thought you were an only child."

"What? No, I'm not. He's five years older than me. So, when the time came, he moved here to New York, but I had no idea he'd be working here, let alone be giving your uncle this job."

"Well, well, well," a familiar voice said behind me. "It's been a long time hasn't it, Leon?"

"Yes, Ryan. It's been two years."

"Oh, come on now. Is that any way to greet your big brother?"

"Well, maybe if you came home more often." I laughed as we gave each other a big hug.

Ryan was wearing a black business suit with a green dress shirt, long black necktie, and black dress shoes.

"Yeah, I'm sorry about that buddy. I've been busy twenty-four seven. Wow! you've gotten a lot stronger since I moved out."

"Wait!" Joe said. "Does that mean he knows your secret, Leon?"

He laughed. "Of course I do. I still have the scars from when he scratched me when we were kids!"

"I said I was sorry!" I laughed, slightly embarrassed.

"Sorry to interrupt, gentlemen," Roy said. "But could we get down to business and talk about this load, please?"

"That's fine, Mr. Vantrice," Ryan said. "Just not here. Connie, set up a conference room for us and make sure we're not disturbed, please?"

"Yes, Mr. Garrett."

After a few minutes in an elevator, we walked into a conference room and sat down ready for the briefing.

"All right, gentlemen," Ryan said. "Let's get down to business. We have a top-secret load that needs to be delivered from a warehouse here in New York City to another DexTech lab in Los Angeles. The company is going to pay you twenty thousand dollars plus expenses, divided four ways for each person on the job: Roy Vantrice and Sid Vantrice will be paid as soon as you get the load to Los Angeles in the form of individualized checks. Joe Vantrice and Leon Garrett will be paid in the form of individualized DexTech scholarships. The four of you have three days to get the load to Los Angeles by six o'clock that night, or there will be no payment. Any questions, gentlemen?"

"I've got a question," Roy said, raising his hand halfway. "I've heard a rumor going around that other truck drivers who've been working for DexTech have had their rigs attacked and destroyed with them barely surviving. Is this true?"

"Attacked?" I exclaimed. "What does he mean by trucks being attacked, Ryan? Do you have any idea who's responsible or why they would attack the trucks?"

"Don't worry, Leon. That is just an unfounded rumor," Ryan said. "Now, if there are no further questions, let's get this ball rolling, gentlemen. Leon, before you go, I need to speak to you for a moment, please."

"What's up, big bro? Is there something wrong?"

"No, Leon. I just wanted you to know I love you and hope you'll be careful out there."

"Thanks, Ryan," I said, giving him one last hug. "I really appreciate it."

As I left the conference room, I could tell Ryan was smiling to cover up a feeling of worry or concern he must have felt for me on the inside, or so I hoped on the inside of my heart back then.

When we got to the warehouse later that night, we saw it was locked up and under guard. As we drove up in Roy's old red-and-silver Kenworth semi-truck up to the main entrance, one of the security guards raised his hand and silently ordered him to stop the truck.

"Let me see your IDs," he said sternly.

"Your boss, Mr. Garrett, sent us," Roy replied as he handed him our ID cards.

"All right," he said, handing them back. "You are to park in front of the trailer and wait in your truck while we inspect the rig and load up the trailer. Is that clear?"

"Yes, sir," Roy said.

"Transport has arrived," he said quietly into his radio.

The doors opened wide as Roy drove the truck into the warehouse and parked in front of the silver box trailer as the security guard instructed.

After an hour of waiting, the security guard came up to the truck and knocked on the driver's side door as if it were the front door of a house.

"Yes, sir?" Roy answered after rolling down his window.

"We're done with our inspections and have the trailer loaded. As soon as we make sure it's secure, you'll be good to go."

"All right," Roy replied. "Thank you, sir."

An alarm started blaring around the warehouse.

"What's going on?" Roy asked.

"I'm not sure yet. Stay here while I go check."

There were the sounds of an explosion and machine guns firing coming from behind the trailer.

"Mr. Vantrice," I called out above the loud noises. "What's going on?"

"There's been a perimeter breach!" the security guard shouted. "Get the truck out of here now!"

"Hang on, boys!" Roy shouted as he rolled up his window while hitting the gas petal to the metal floor of the cab.

Roy's truck crashed through the doors of the warehouse and made a sharp right onto the main road.

"Sorry about that!" he shouted out the window. "Send me the bill!"

He adjusted his rearview mirror.

"Hey Leon? Joe? Sid? You boys all right, back there?" he asked us as he laughed.

All we could do is sit there, frozen with fear while clinging on to our seats.

Meanwhile, what we didn't realize was three bumbling yet disgruntled ex-employees of DexTech—Ned, a super strong yet dimwitted giant of a man; Tim, a tall, thin, timid man yet a genius-level computer hacker; and Sam, a short, foul-tempered conman and the leader of the trio—were the ones responsible for trying to break into the warehouse to steal the load from us.

"Ned, you idiot!" Sam shouted. "You were supposed to stop the truck from getting away!"

"Sorry, boss," Ned replied, scratching his head. "You told me to beat up bad guys."

"Yes. Beat up bad guys, and don't let the truck get away!"

"Now, now, now, Sam," Tim said. "Be nice. Ned just did what he thought you told him to do."

"Can it, geek for brains!" Sam shouted. "If you had just disabled the warehouse's security system, we would've gotten that truck and been rich!"

As the trio started arguing amongst each other, a cold, silent figure finally made his presence known by firing a blue and white beam at them that barely missed them by inches of their faces and hit a nearby wall, which froze it into solid ice.

"Gentlemen!" he said coolly. "Perhaps I can be of some assistance?"

"Who the heck are you?" Sam demanded.

"The name's Coldwave, a man who's in the same boat as you. But unlike you, I have a way to find them, and you have a way to follow them."

"Really?" Sam said sternly. "How?"

"Because as the truck was leaving. I put a tracking device on the back of the trailer"

"What's in it for us?" Sam asked.

"I have a target I need to kill," he said with a smirk. "That's all I want. You three can have the reward for all I care."

A security guard regained consciousness, grabbed his gun, and pointed it at the four intruders.

"Freeze!" he shouted after getting up on his feet.

Within a split second, the cold figure fires and a large icicle impaled him in the chest and freezes him from the inside out.

"Ooh, bad choice of words." He smirked. "So, gentlemen, do we have a deal?"

Sam shook his hand while sharing a jaw-dropped look on his face with Tim and Ned.

He smirked. "Good. I'll be waiting in the car if you need me."

"Let's go, boys," Sam ordered, finally breaking their silence.

The next day after we escaped the warehouse attack, we were passing through Las Vegas and entering the Great Basin Desert. Roy claimed we were in the home stretch to making it to Los Angeles. Although Sid was starting to get paranoid we were not going to make our deadline in time, and it was starting to worry me as well. Well, at least I didn't have to worry about anyone discovering my secret identity as Leoman, because the only people who knew this were my family and Joe, Sid, and Roy, who were riding with me.

"Come on, Dad!" Sid started fussing. "We're going to be late!"

"Relax, boy," Roy said calmly. "We'll make it and get paid."

"But Mr. Vantrice," I said, "we still have another six hours or so before we get to Los Angeles."

"Don't worry, Leon," Joe said, trying to calm me down. "For all we know, Sid may have miscalculated because of the time zone change. We're still good on time."

"No, I did not!" Sid said before muttering to himself. "But it will be a miracle if we get there on time at this rate."

"What's that, boy?" Roy shouted sarcastically. "You say I should go slower?"

"No, sir," Sid said, trying to cover up his last comment.

"Well, then," Roy said, "hush your mouth and stop whining. We'll be there on time."

"Yes, sir," he said, finally sitting in his seat quietly.

I heard my phone vibrate with a call from Annie.

"Hey, Annie," I answered on the phone. "What's up?"

"Hey, Leon," she replied. "How are the college visits going with your brother?"

"College visits?" I asked loud enough so Joe could hear me and hoping he would help me out.

"Yeah," Annie said. "Your parents told Mr. Jacobs and our school you and Joe were going on college visits with Uncle Roy and your brother."

"I don't know what to say to her!" I mouthed to Joe.

"It must be our cover!" Joe mouthed back. "Just go with it!"

"Leon?" she asked. "Are you still there?"

"Oh, yeah," I said. "Yeah, the college visits are going great."

"That's good," she said as I breathed a quiet sigh of relief. "Anyway, I wanted to call you and let you know I missed you."

"Aww, I miss you too, Annie. I'm sorry you couldn't come with us."

"Me too," Annie said. "I wish we could hang out together. But Rachel's been dragging me around the city for Leoman sightings."

"Leoman sightings, huh?" I asked. "Well, I wish Joe and I could join you."

"Yeah," Annie said with a chuckle. "Well, I better let you get back to your college visits."

"Uh, yeah," I sighed. "I hope to see you when we get back."

"Me too," Annie said. "See you then, Leon. Bye."

"Bye, Annie," I said, ending the call while feeling sad about it on the inside.

"You okay?" Joe asked.

"Yeah." I sighed. "I hope."

We felt the loud bang sound of something ramming into the back of the trailer.

"Whoa!" Sid exclaimed. "What the heck was that?"

"Well, boys," Roy said as he stuck his head out his window, "looks like we've got some company. Hang on!"

I looked out the rearview mirror and saw what looked like four guys Ned, Tim, and Sam, riding in a heavily modified Ford Model A that had been turned into a customized hot rod dune buggy. It was black with orange flames. A big, muscular man was driving, while a tall, skinny man had a laptop computer and was sitting on the front passenger seat. The other two men were sitting in the two back seats as if they were being driven in a limousine. Even though I couldn't hear what they were saying, I could still read their lips.

"Come on, Ned!" their apparent leader said excitedly. "Get them! Stop that truck by any means necessary!"

"Be careful, now," said his passenger. "We don't want to ruin the cargo inside the trailer."

"Hey!" the leader said sternly. "Don't tell me or my boys what to do! That's my job!"

"Better watch your tone with me, Sammy boy," said his passenger. "You don't want me to lose my cool now, do you?"

"No, no, no!" the leader stammered. "We're cool! We're cool! No freezing necessary!"

"Good boy," his passenger smirked. "Now, get me closer to that trailer. My target should be out of the truck any minute."

"Yes, sir," the leader grumbled.

As soon as their car came within inches of the trailer, the passenger used his ice blasts as a form of propulsion and leapt onto the top of it. He managed to stay on the trailer due to magnetic treads on his boots, which still allowed him to move like an average person does on a sidewalk. As he started making his way to the truck cab, I made a split-second decision to change into my Leoman costume. Seeing I had no other choice, I rolled down the passenger side window down and flipped outside the window, landing onto the trailer. I used the claws in the nailbeds of my feet to stay on the trailer while extending the claws in my finger nailbeds to fight Coldwave. Thankfully, I didn't tear holes in my gloves and boots, as Joe had installed tiny openings in the fingers of the gloves and the fronts of the boots for my claws to extend out of them.

"What the …?" Sid exclaimed. "Leon's Leoman?"

"Yes," Joe said sternly. "And you better not tell anyone. Understand?"

"Yeah, yeah." Sid quivered. "I understand."

I refocused my attention on our mysterious hijacker.

"So we finally meet, Leoman," he smirked.

"Who are you?" I demanded. "And what do you want?"

"I've been hired for one reason: to find you, Leoman—and to freeze your heart cold in ice!"

He used his icy powers to create a razor-sharp shard and threw it at me as if it were a throwing knife. Thanks to my catlike reflexes, I caught the shard with one hand and crushed it.

Realizing neither one of us was going to back down, with a smirk, he created more shards and threw them at me as well but more quickly. Even though some of them nicked me, I managed to evade most of them.

"Hey!" I shouted, seeing the nicks and tears in my costume. "Not cool! Do you know how much this costume costs to maintain?"

"Well, send me the bill, Mr. Feline Schmuck!" He smirked.

I tried to charge at him with my claws scratching his chest in the style of a right cross.

"Ha! How do you like it?"

He made a makeshift icepack that stuck to his chest, while making an icicle the size and length of a spear.

"You're gonna pay for that, feline freak!" he shouted as he tried to make an enraged jab at me with his ice spear.

As we fought on top of the trailer, Sam finally lost his patience with Coldwave and decided to take matters into his own hands.

"Ned, pull over to the left side of the trailer and hit it as hard as you can!" he ordered.

"But, boss," Ned said, concerned. "Mr. Coldwave's still fighting Leoman up there!"

"Just do it, you nitwit!" he shouted.

"Okay, boss," Ned said obediently.

We felt a huge slam of metal hitting metal. Their hotrod car made the whole trailer shake beneath Coldwave and me as if we were in an earthquake and almost tipped the trailer off its wheels.

"Roy!" I shouted, turning my head away for a split second. "Keep the truck and trailer stable!"

But as I turned my head back to face him, there was a painful squishing sound from my abdomen. Coldwave had just impaled me with his ice spear, and it was starting to freeze me from the inside out. He threw me and his ice spear off the trailer, where I landed on my back ten feet away from the road with the hard crunch of pavement and gravel. I tried getting up, but being impaled and because of the two different temperature extremes of the hot sand and the ice spear, I wasn't sure If I was going to survive even with my healing abilities.

As I gazed at the truck with my friends, still trying to drive away from Coldwave and the three goons, I found myself starting to pass out from my injuries yet again. But just before I did, I saw what I thought was the mysterious Boy in White.

"You have to get up," he said. "You have to get up and fight like the lion I know you are."

The next thing I knew, I woke up still in the exact spot where I landed.

"What the …?" I said as I quickly got to my feet.

I was shocked to see I was still miraculously alive and my costume was fixed as if nothing had happened to me.

"Wow!" I said to myself. "Who is that little boy in white?"

I remembered what had happened and immediately began tracking the truck by using my lion-like senses to follow the smell of diesel fuel. I was surprised to find the scent was only an hour or two old. As I followed them running on all fours like a jungle cat, I was hoping and praying Joe and the others were still alive and all the while was still trying to figure out how I managed to be impaled and still be alive.

CHAPTER 10
WHAT IS THE PRICE OF BETRAYING FAMILY?

While I was tracking my friends, the sun had set, and the midafternoon had turned into night as Coldwave, and the trio of thugs had managed to hijack the truck and trailer. They also took Joe, Roy, and Sid as hostages. When they finally got to a nearby truck stop, they tied up their hostages and left them sitting on the ground next to the truck while Sam got on his phone and started to demand a ransom from the CEO of DexTech.

"That's right, Doc!" he said into his phone arrogantly. "I want one million dollars sent to my bank account right now, or you'll never see this load or the drivers again!"

"Shouldn't we see what's in the trailer first?" Coldwave asked.

"Well ..." Sam said before stopping himself to think for a minute. "Yes ... yes, we should do that! Ned, Tim, open up the trailer, now!"

"Yes, boss," they both said in unison.

They ran to the back of the trailer and tried to open it.

"Step aside, gentlemen." Coldwave sighed after watching their unsuccessful attempts.

They dived out of the way just as he blasted at the trailer's lock, freezing it in solid ice. He then shattered it with a single flick of his finger.

"It's all yours, gentlemen." He smirked to himself as he turned and walked away from the trailer.

"Well," Sam said, breaking the stunned silence once again. "What are you two waiting for, Christmas? Open the door and let's see what's inside!"

When they finally opened the door, they stared in confusion as they discovered the mystery load they hijacked was three prisoners locked in three high-tech holding cells and were in an artificial form of sleep.

"Hey! What gives?" Sam shouted in disgust and disappointment. "Ned! Grab one of the hostages! We need answers, now!"

"Okay, boss," he said, grabbing Joe with one arm and dragging him over to the back of the trailer.

"Did you know about this?" Sam shouted while Ned held Joe's head up to make him look inside the trailer.

"What?" Joe exclaimed. "No way!"

"You're lying!" Sam shouted. "How can you possibly not know what you're transporting?"

"It was a top-secret load!" Roy said. "How were we supposed to know?"

"Uh, actually, Uncle Roy," Sid said quietly with a nervous chuckle. "They kind of told me about it, heh-heh."

"What?" Joe shouted. "You knew about this?"

"Why didn't you tell us, boy?" Roy said.

"Because there was money at stake!" Sid shouted.

"You betrayed us, boy!" Roy shouted. "You betrayed family just to save your own skin!"

"Betrayed family?" Sid shouted. "You're kidding me, right? Some of our ancestors were in the Italian mafia! There's not honor in this family whatsoever, Roy!"

"I really hate to interrupt this little family drama." Coldwave smirked. "But I'm going to need someone smart enough to help me get these superhumans out of this trailer."

"Hey, wait a minute!" Sam said. "That's my score! I mean, our score!"

"That's right!" Tim chimed in. "You said you didn't care what this score was as long as you killed your target! Namely, Leoman!"

"Well, that was before I found out what the load was," Coldwave said.

"Back off while you still can," Sam said sternly.

"And who's going to stop me?" Coldwave remarked while raising his hands. "You three?"

"No!" I roared as I finally made it to the truck stop and surprised them. "But I will."

"Impossible! I killed you!" Coldwave shouted.

"Well," I said with a smirk, shrugging my shoulders, "I guess I heal faster than we both thought."

"Take this!" Coldwave said, enraged, as he created and threw his ice shards at me once again.

This time, I managed to evade all of them because I was prepared for his reaction of seeing me still alive.

"Ha! Is that all you've got?" I laughed while evading more of his ice shards.

"Hold still, you feline freak, and I'll show you!" Coldwave shouted, enraged that he kept missing his target.

When I got close enough, he tried to make an ice shield. But my claws were sharp to slice it in half and scratch his face. Thankfully, Joe had taught me how to have some finesse when using them in combat during our training lessons at Roy's gym.

"Aah!" Coldwave yelled with pain as stumbled back a couple of steps. "You little fuzz-faced creep!"

Just as I thought, he resorted to creating the ice spear just like the last time we fought. But this time, when he charged at me with it, I evaded it without even a glance. I broke it in half with one hit and shoved him five feet away with a light push to his chest.

While Coldwave was busy getting back up from landing on his back, Joe had managed to break through his restraints and free himself. He got in the truck and started it up. But as he tried to drive it away from the fighting, Ned, Tim, and Sam were hiding in the back of the cab and decided to take back their hostage.

"Going somewhere, boy?" Sam asked with a big sarcastic grin while holding a gun near Joe's face.

They forced him out of the truck where I could see them in plain view.

"Hey, Leoman!" Sam shouted. "Let us all go, or your friend here gets a bullet in his head!"

"Joe!" I shouted, fearing for his life.

"Don't worry about me, Leoman!" Joe shouted. "I can take care of myself!"

Joe knocked the gun out of Sam's hand and kicked it away from them.

"All right, Joe!" I shouted joyfully.

"You take care of Coldwave, Leoman! I've got these three stooges!"

"You got it, Joe!" I replied in agreement.

But just as I was about to knock out Coldwave and end our fight, there was a huge flash of light which drew my attention away from him. Apparently, I had been so focused on our fight that I didn't notice three heavily armed military helicopters had appeared until they flashed one of their spotlights on the ground. Which made me realize it was time for me to make a hasty exit away from the scene and sneak back into the truck. I dropped Coldwave and leapt away before the astonished pilots could take a shot at me. It looked as if my friends had more trouble as I looked from inside the truck and saw climbing ropes being dropped from the sides of them with soldiers armed with M4 machine guns sliding the ropes. As we were soon surrounded by them, one of the soldiers radioed from the ground to his superior still in the helicopter.

"Area secure, sir. I repeat, area secure."

"Roger that, Corporal," said the pilot. "Agent V is on his way down."

"Copy that," he replied. "Department of Superhuman Investigations, look sharp!"

Their superior came out of the helicopter just as it landed. He was complete covered in black and dark gray military equipment, and strangely enough, he was wearing a ski mask with goggles to completely cover his facial features and even his hair color from being discovered by prying eyes. The lenses of his goggles were so tinted, I couldn't see his eyes even with my animal-keen senses.

"At ease, Corporal," he ordered calmly. He turned his attention toward my friends. "Now, which one of you gentlemen is Sid Vantrice?"

"He is, sir," Joe said, pointing him out as he tried to sneak away out of trouble yet again.

"Mr. Vantrice! Stay right where you are!"

"Yes, sir!" he replied nervously. "You don't have to worry about me at all!"

"Now, which one is Roy Vantrice?" he asked.

"I am, sir."

"I'm Agent V. We're with the Department of Superhuman Investigations. Is this your rig, Mr. Vantrice?"

"Yes, sir."

"Could you open up the trailer, please, Mr. Vantrice?"

"Yes, sir."

After Roy opened the trailer doors, Agent V jumped into the trailer and inspected the villains and saw they were still in their cells and, more importantly, still in artificial sleep.

"Packages are still here," he said with approval as he jumped out of the trailer. "All right, let's pack them back up and move out!"

"Now wait a darn minute!" Roy said, frustrated. "I drove this rig from coast to coast, and we still haven't been paid for a load we didn't know could kill us!"

"Don't worry, Mr. Vantrice. Mr. Garrett has reassured me you and your crew will still be compensated—other than Sid Vantrice, of course."

"Wait, what?" Sid shouted. "What do you mean except for me?"

"Because, Mr. Vantrice," Agent V explained, "as the broker, you were supposed to make sure the load arrived safely at DexTech. Therefore, you don't get paid."

"This is ridiculous!" Sid shouted as he stomped back into the truck.

"Well, we'd like to get going," Roy said, "but the safety seals on the trailer doors are damaged beyond repair. There's no way to close them without your prisoners falling out."

"Don't worry, Mr. Vantrice," I said, chiming in as I climbed on top of the truck. "I'll hold them while you drive."

"All right, then," he said. "As soon as we get to DexTech, you're free to go, Leoman."

"Thank you, sir. Wait. How do you know my name?"

"DSI!" he shouted to the soldiers, ignoring my question. "Let's move out! Leoman is to be treated as a nonhostile! As soon as we get to DexTech, you will let him go free! Do I make myself clear?"

"Sir, yes, sir!" they all responded.

They shut the trailer doors and I climbed onto the back of it and managed to hold them closed all the way to the DexTech lab in Los Angeles in the same night.

When we got there, Ryan was waiting for us looking worried. Probably for our safety as well as the safety of our load.

"Hey!" he called out. "Is everyone all right? Where's Leon?"

"He's all right, Ryan," Joe whispered. "We snuck him into the truck so he could change out of his suit."

"Okay, good. Thank the Lord."

"Mr. Garrett!" Agent V called out. "We've found no trace of your brother's whereabouts. I'm sorry, but I'm afraid he's MIA."

"No, I'm not!" I called out from the truck. "I was hiding in the truck trying to call the police when those goons hijacked the truck!"

"Oh, Leon!" Ryan said, giving me a big hug. "Thank heaven you're okay!"

"I already did," I said with a slight chuckle.

"I'm glad you're okay too, Leon," Roy said, "but we still need to get paid so we can get home."

"Don't worry, Mr. Vantrice," Ryan said as he handed him a check.

"You've all upheld your end of the deal, except for Sid. Do whatever you want with him."

"Thank you, Mr. Garrett." Roy smiled and chuckled. "We will do just that, sir."

"You're welcome," Ryan said to Roy before turning to me. "Well, little brother, it looks like we're parting ways again."

"Yes, it does Ryan." I sighed sadly. "I hope we see each other soon, Ryan."

"Same here, Leon." We gave each other one last hug.

We turned our backs to each other, with Ryan going inside the DexTech facility and me walking back to the truck to get ready for the long trip back to Sedalia City, Indiana.

"Are you okay?" Joe asked as I climbed into the truck.

"Yeah, I will be. I'm going to miss him, though."

"I know what you mean, buddy. I know what you mean."

Meanwhile, when Ryan reached his small, temporary office, he found he had an unexpected visitor waiting for him in the dark room as he turned on the light switch.

"Agent V, I really wish you'd stop doing that," he said, surprisingly unfazed.

"And I wish you wouldn't keep so many secrets from DSI," Agent V replied as he sat on a chair behind the door. "After all, knowing about potential superhuman threats is why I get aid the big bucks."

"What are you talking about?" Ryan asked.

"I'm talking about your younger brother—Leon, is it?" Agent V asked. "Or should I say, the so-called Leoman from Sedalia City, Indiana?"

"If you say a word to any of your superiors," Ryan said, "I'll make sure DexTech will never do business with DSI again!"

"Now, calm down, Mr. Garrett," Agent V said. "Your family's secret is safe with DSI as long as we keep our present relationship."

"All right, Agent," Ryan said. "What does DSI want now?"

"Well, besides your brother to join DSI," Agent V said.

"Which will never happen if I have my way!" Ryan exclaimed.

"We've recently had one of our large prototypes stolen," Agent V said.

"Which one?" Ryan asked, shocked.

"The energy converter," Agent V said. You know, the one that was found in the wreckage of Dr. Kingston's residence and made into an improved prototype copy?"

"How was it stolen?" Ryan exclaimed. "We've had our security teams keep an eye on it since it was created!"

"Well, Mr. Garrett," Agent V said. "It was your technicians and your security teams. Do you have an explanation?"

"Only one," Ryan sighed.

"Mind-Breaker and the Dark Claw Syndicate?" Agent V asked.

"Yes," Ryan said. "I mean, who else could?"

"We'll figure out who's a double agent later," Agent V reassured him. "In the meantime, we've got bigger problems to worry about, and so does your brother."

"God in heaven help us all," Ryan said quietly as he looked out the window, worrying not only about me but for the health and safety of everyone in Sedalia City. "Please be safe, Leon. Be safe."

Meanwhile, deep below Ryan's office in the DexTech lab, the sinister figure of Mind-Breaker appeared and easily dispatched all the technicians and security guards without triggering any alarms. He went over to where the young man once known as the Human Hydra lay in the coma Mind-Breaker had himself put him in. He did something he had rarely done in his life. As he fixed his mind, he injected him with a more powerful version of the FANG formula, turning him into the Human Hydra once again.

"W-what's going on?" he asked as he awoke from his coma.

"I'm giving you one last chance," Mind-Breaker said. "Kill Leoman and all will be forgiven. Fail me again, and it will be the last time I will fix what I have broken."

"When do we start, then?" he asked with an evil smile.

CHAPTER 11
HOW DOES SID GET REVENGE?

It had been a month after we got back from our cross-country trip for DexTech, and I have to say, it was not a great point in my life. I was so sad and depressed all the time that I felt as if it would never end. Because I still had to keep my secret from one of the closest people I had to friends. Annie: she deserved so much better than me in every shape and form, but we were growing further and further apart every day since I got back. On top of that, the Vantrice family disowned Sid after what he did on the trip. So, not only do we not have a trusted informant, but we also had no leads on either the sinister and elusive Mind-Breaker or his plans.

Thankfully, I still had Joe as a close friend. He tried to cheer me up by taking me to see a football game involving our favorite team, the Sedalia City Braves, at Luigi Stadium. Unfortunately, it worked only a little bit to cure the depression in my heart.

"Oh, come on, Leon!" Joe exclaimed finally having enough of it. "How can you still be such a sourpuss when the Braves are winning!"

"Hmm?" I asked, coming out of my deep thoughts. "Oh, I'm sorry, Joe."

"Seriously, you've got to get over Annie," he said, pouting.

"How am I supposed to get over Annie? Besides you, she's been one of my closest friends for years!"

The sound of Joe's phone started vibrating in his pocket.

"Who is it?" I asked. "Mr. Jacobs?"

"No, it's my Uncle Roy," Joe said. He read the text. "'Joe, DSI found out about Leon! Find him and both of you meet us at the gym ASAP! Don't tell anyone about this until we meet afterwards!'"

We left the stadium and went to the parking lot where we got in our old friend known to us as the hippie van. From there, Joe drove us nonstop to Roy's fighting gym as we tried to figure out how DSI found out Leon Garrett is Leoman.

When we finally arrived, we found it strange that there was not a sound coming from inside the gym. As we opened the doors to the front entrance, we discovered the whole place had been ransacked! The mirrors were smashed, and the benches were broken in half.

"Uncle Roy?" Joe called out. "Uncle Roy! Where are you?"

"There he is!" I exclaimed, spotting him face down underneath some fallen debris.

"Quick, let's get him out from under there!" he exclaimed as he ran over to him and pulled him out while I used my lion strength to move the debris off him.

We flipped him onto his back and tried to revive him.

"Uncle Roy, can you hear me?" Joe asked as he shook him once. "Leon, please tell me he isn't dead!"

"Don't worry, Joe," I said calmly as I leaned my head into his chest. "I can hear his heartbeat. He's alive but unconscious."

"Oh, thank the Lord!" Joe sighed with relief. "But who would do something like this?"

"Sid … Sid," Roy said weakly as he tried to sit up.

"What?" Joe asked shocked. "Who did this, Uncle Roy?"

"It was Sid—him and that snake guy you fought a while back," he said before passing out once again.

"I can't believe it!" Joe said. "That lousy, stinking son of a gun!"

"What, Joe?" I exclaimed.

"It was Sid! It was Sid! The little rat sold us out!"

"We've got to get out of here and call my dad!" I said as we started to carry Roy out the door together.

"You better believe we're going to get out of here all right!" Joe shouted. "Because as soon as we get Uncle Roy out of here, I'm going to find Sid and give him the beating of his life!"

"Calm down, Joe. As soon as we get Roy to a hospital, we'll both go search for Sid."

The doors slammed shut, leaving us in the dark for a split second until the lights came on!

"Oh, I'm afraid you two won't be making it to the hospital today!" said Sid as he came up behind us. He was dressed in a dark grey T-shirt with a black leather jacket over it as well as dark blue jeans and black boots.

"Sid, you little rat!" Joe shouted. "How could you do this to Uncle Roy? Your own flesh and blood family?"

"Family means nothing to me now!" Sid shouted.

"We won't let you get away with this, Sid!"

"Oh, I'm afraid there's nothing even you can do about it now, Leon," Sid chuckled. "Or should I say, Leoman!"

Another familiar figure walked out from behind the shadows!

"Well, Leoman," Human Hydra said with an evil smile, "what do you say, runt! Are you finally ready for the final round of our showdown?"

He was back to being in his snakelike form, but he was physically bigger and a lot more muscular.

"Joe, take Roy and get out of here, now!" I said.

"Wait, what about you?"

"Costume or no costume, I have to finish this once and for all! Now go!"

"All right," Joe sighed calmly as he turned away while carrying Roy. "But I'm coming back! Because this isn't over, Sid!"

"Actually, cousin," Sid said as he pulled a gun out. "I think it is."

"Joe! Look out!" I shouted as he turned to face me.

Bang! Sid shot Joe square in the middle of his chest.

"Nooooo!" I screamed in horror as Joe dropped to the ground.

I couldn't believe it. I couldn't believe my eyes. Sid had just shot Joe!

With the rage and sorrow of Joe being shot boiling in my veins, I launched myself at Sid. But before I could get to Sid, Human Hydra and his copies grabbed me and wrestled me to the ground.

"He's all yours, Human Hydra!" Sid laughed as he casually walked out the back entrance. "Oh, and Leon? If Joe's still alive over there, tell him I was the one who killed Jamie, would you, pal?"

As I struggled with all my lion strength to break free of his copies' grip, the original Human Hydra walked over to me with what looked like a big, long syringe in his hand.

"Before we kill you, Leoman," he said with an evil smile, "we have a little present for you courtesy of the Mind-Breaker!"

He slammed the point of the syringe into my shoulder and injected what I can only assume was a toxin made from the FANG formula into me. I felt so drowsy and my body felt weak. I felt like I could barely stand on my own.

"W-w-what did y-you do to me?" I stammered in a daze, feeling I was about to pass out.

"How does it feel, Leoman?" he asked mockingly before he punched me. "How does it feel to be just a normal human? To have no powers?"

He grabbed me and tossed me across the room. I landed with a big thud against a nearby wall as some boards broke behind me. As he walked over laughing at me as he came closer and closer to me, he grabbed me by my torn shirt and as he was about to lift me off the ground.

"So much for the big hero!" He laughed, preparing to blast me with his acidic saliva by inhaling a huge breath.

But as he did, I summoned every ounce of strength I had left and jerked my head down to duck away from the blast. I had narrowly missed him burning me alive.

Unfortunately, the blast hit an exposed gas main in the wall, which exploded in his face and killed him almost instantly. The only thing left of him was a blackened mass of cloth and snake scales, which I saw through my blurry eyes. By the grace of God, I had managed to barely miss the explosion because Human Hydra tossed me aside to protect himself even in my weakened state. But as I climbed out of the rubble, I noticed that Joe was missing! I tried to search for him. I noticed a black figure in my blurry vision that looked a lot like Agent V from the DSI, dragging Joe and Roy out of the nearby rubble and out the front entrance. As I staggered out the same entrance, he leaned them both side by side onto the side of the door just outside the building before disappearing from my sight. I reached into Joe's pants, grabbed his phone, and called 911. I stayed with them until the ambulance arrived and rode in it with Joe all the way to the hospital.

A few hours later, I was standing in a hallway outside of Joe's hospital room, trying to watch over him and praying on the inside for God to save his life. Just as I was about to walk away, Annie came up to me and stood quietly right next to me.

"How is he?" she asked softly.

"He just got out of surgery. But the doctors say he's still in critical condition and it'll take a miracle for him to pull through."

"Oh, Leon." She started to cry and hugged me. "I'm so sorry about Joe. I know how close you two are."

"Thanks, Annie." I sighed as we let go of each other.

"How are you holding up?"

"Honestly, not very well," I said sadly as I cried. "Because I know it's my fault one of my best friends is going to die, and I can't do anything about it."

"I know. It's okay. But don't worry. The doctors are going to do everything they can to save Joe."

"I'm sorry, Annie," I said with tears falling down my face, "but you really don't know what I've done and what I've dragged Joe into."

"What do you mean?"

"Annie, there's something I have to tell you," I said in a serious tone while wiping the tears away from my watery eyes. I finally plucked up the courage to tell her something I'd been hiding from her for a long time.

"Okay, Leon," she said almost impatiently. "If this is about any feelings you've got for me, then—"

"I'm Leoman," I interrupted her.

"Wait, what?" she said surprised.

"You heard me," I said. "I. Am. Leoman."

"Okay," Annie sighed "I think you're imaging yourself being Leoman."

"Annie," I said sternly, "I'm serious."

"Oh, yeah?" Annie said. "If you're Leoman, prove it."

"I can't."

"What did you say?"

"I can't, Annie."

"Why?"

"Because."

"Leon, why can't you prove to me that you're Leoman?" she asked as if pressuring me.

"Because I don't have my powers anymore, okay?" I snapped at her. "I lost my powers when Human Hydra put some kind of toxin in me, and now, I don't even know if I'll ever get them back!"

"You're serious!" She gasped as she saw the look in my eyes. "You really are Leoman! I can't believe it! Why didn't you tell me? Why have you been hiding this from me?"

"Because I promised my parents' I wouldn't tell anyone when I got their blessing."

"I'm one of your best friends!" she exclaimed. "And you didn't trust me enough to tell me that you fight crime and save lives in a superhero costume as an extracurricular activity?"

"I'm sorry, Annie! But can we talk about this when we get to my car so I can take you home, please?"

After a while, we went out to my car so I could drive her home to her parents—and that's when we swerved around the Boy in White and ended up as patients in the hospital.

Now everything had come full circle to me, bleeding on the hospital floor and dying from my injuries because I had tried to be a superhero without my powers. For those who are not Batman and do not have powers, please don't try it at home, or you will end up where I was at right back then. It's funny. The last person I could only think of was Annie and how much I want to tell her I loved her. Despite everything that had happened between us, I wanted to say the words "I love you" to her before I died.

As if I were drifting off into heaven from the hospital floor, I saw the Boy in White again. Although this time around, he was glowing white as freshly fallen snow sparkling from the sun's rays.

"Get up," he said. "Get up, Leoman. God's not finished with you yet."

"God?" I asked faintly. "What do you mean God's not finished with me yet?"

"God still has a mission for you to do. You have to stop Mind-Breaker and save Annie. Before he can turn God's children into monstrous beasts."

"How can I save Annie without my powers?"

"I've removed the toxin inhibiting your leonine abilities," he said as he held the muddy green liquid. "Now come on! Stand up, Leoman! Stand up and fight like the lion He knows you are! I'll be there if you need my help again! But for now, wake up! Wake up now!"

I woke up on the hospital floor, gasping for the air to fill in my lungs. I could honestly not believe it! Besides a slight feeling of dizziness, I felt strong. I felt healthy. Best of all, I felt fully and completely alive again!

Just as I was getting myself up, Agent V and his squad of DSI agents came marching into the hallway, and as they all surrounded me, I saw Agent V's arm extend to help me back up to my feet. I grabbed it, and I still couldn't believe that a few minutes ago, I was almost dead!

"Are you all right, Mr. Garrett?"

"Surprisingly, yes I am!"

"Good," he said before taking a serious tone. "Because we need Leoman, now!"

"Why would you be asking me? I don't know who he is!"

"Because we're the Department of Superhuman Investigations," he said sarcastically. "We know everything there is to know about emerging superhumans, such as the shadowy man who took over protecting Salemburg after you and your family moved here."

"Wait a minute! You mean I'm not the only one?"

"Of course you know that's classified information. But so are these."

He pulled two small sealed vials out from one of his belt pouches and handed them to me.

"These two vials of anti-FANG serum are for you—one to inoculate yourself and the other to neutralize the FANG formula gas Mind-Breaker is planning to release from the Baker Chemical Plant."

"Thank you, sir," I said as I stored them in my belt pouches. "I'll try to be careful with them."

"As soon as you neutralize the gas and defeat Mind-Breaker," he said as he continued briefing me. "We'll move and arrest Mind-Breaker and start curing the mutated populace."

"Don't worry, sir. I will, but what about Joe? Is he going to be okay?"

"I promise you, Leon. We'll do whatever it takes to help save Joe's life to the best of our capabilities."

"All right, Agent V. I'll work with you, for now at least."

"Very well," Agent V said, satisfied with my terms. "Welcome to DSI, Leoman. All right, let's move out, agents!"

Before we got to the chemical plant I changed into my costume, feeling thankful to be wearing it as Leoman again. When we got there, the Sedalia City Police Department was there in full swing, with their spotlights shining and shifting around in the gathering darkness of the night from their cars and helicopters. They were shining them all around the facility but mainly focused on the smokestacks and silos. As they were the most likely parts of the facility where he would disperse the FANG formula as a widespread spray, the police and the National Guard were ready to blow them up if Mind-Breaker tried to use them. We approached the chemical plant's main entrance and stood alongside the authorities.

"Agent V!" called out the sudden voice of my dad, coming up from behind us. "What's DSI doing here? And why is Leoman with you?"

"Don't worry, Captain Garrett," Agent V reassured him. "Leoman's back on duty with a clean bill of health, all courtesy of DSI's medical team."

"Is this true, Leoman?" he asked, turning his attention toward me.

"Yes, it is, Captain Garrett," I said while keeping my secret identity in front of Agent V.

"You see?" Agent V said. "Now, if you'll excuse us, Leoman and DSI have a city to save."

After he turned his face away from us, Dad quietly got my attention so we could speak privately.

"Hey! Leoman!" He called out and motioned for me to walk over and talk to him.

"What's wrong, Dad?" I asked him quietly.

"Are you sure you're okay? Because last I heard, you and Annie were just in the hospital an hour ago."

"Don't worry, Dad. I got my powers back due to divine intervention."

"What do you mean?"

"I'll explain later, sir. But right now, Mind-Breaker has Annie and I've got to save her."

"Wait, what? Leoman!" he exclaimed as I started to turn and walk away from him.

"Don't worry, Captain Garrett! I'll make sure she comes out safely!"

I caught up to Agent V as he and the DSI agents were about to break into the front entrance. I stood to the left of Agent V as they were breaking the padlocked doors, nervously wondering what evil monstrosities of Mind-Breaker's awaited us inside.

"Don't worry, Leoman," Agent V said calmly. "We're going to get Annie back. I promise."

"Sorry, sir. It's just … I have always had my best friend by side during situations like this. I just hope and pray your medical teams can save his life."

"Relax, Leoman. If Joe's still as tough as he once was, he'll be too stubborn to die so easily."

"Really? How do you know Joe so well?"

"Because." He sighed as he pulled off his mask, revealing his face underneath as he shook out his long black hair and wiping the sweat off his pale brow. "He's my brother."

"Wait, *what*?" I exclaimed, shocked at who he was. "Your brother! That means … you're Jamie Vantrice! But … but that's impossible! You're supposed to be dead! You died in Joe's arms that night during that gang war with the Scorchers!"

"That's true," he said calmly. "To the world at large, little Jamie Vantrice is dead—and Agent V of DSI stands in his place now."

"But … but Sid said he killed you!" I stammered. "How are you even alive?"

"He almost did. But DSI managed to revive me and replaced my body with a fake when they secretly recruited me."

"Recruited you? For what?"

"So I could keep an eye on you. To take your place protecting this city should you die … And to kill you should you lose control of the animal inside you."

"Well, you can tell your superiors this! I'm more human than they think I am! You should be the one to tell Joe you're still alive!"

"We've broken through the lock, sir!" one of the agents called out to break up our intense argument.

"Look, I'm sorry, Leoman. But this has to be a kept secret, especially from Joe."

"You know what, Jamie?" I said, enraged. "You shouldn't keep those kinds of secrets, especially from your family!"

As I walked ahead of the group through the opened entrance, the room was only lighted from the outside. We walked into the dark room with the agents having their guns drawn and I having my claws unsheathed, ready to fight at a moment's notice. Just as we thought the coast was clear, we heard a low growling like mine.

"Leoman, was that you?" Agent V asked quietly.

"No, I'm afraid it wasn't me this time."

"Indeed, it wasn't Leoman," Sid said mockingly with an almost inhuman growl as he came charging from out of the darkness.

As we spun around to face him, we stared up in horror at the monstrous lion-like beast that was once the sniveling and cowardly Sid. Apparently, in exchange for betraying Joe and me, Mind-Breaker promised him a form of the FANG formula, making him a large, muscular lion-like body and razor-sharp claws.

"Sid?" I asked in shock.

"Sorry, Sid's not here right now," he said, chuckling evilly. "The name's Nemean and I am now the Dark Leoman!"

"Sid, do you have any idea what you have done to yourself?" I said, almost begging him to come back to his senses.

"Yes, I do, Leon!" he said, laughing. "I've become someone who never has to hide behind anyone else for protection ever again!"

"Sid Vantrice!" Agent V shouted while he and the other DSI raised their guns to Sid's head. "You are ordered to stand down, or we will be forced to shoot!"

"Ha! As if those puny toy guns are going to hurt me!"

"That does it!" Agent V said. "Open fire, agents!"

"No, *wait*!" I shouted, trying to stop them.

But it was too late. Agent V and his agents had succeeded only in making him angry without making a scratch on his body, leaving only minor bruises. As he started to charge at us at full speed, I was honestly thinking two things as I tried to block his advance at the time. The first thing was this is going to hurt—a lot. And the second thing was, I hope I can survive this fight.

Just before the impact, I was seeing darkness. Nothing but darkness. I felt a hard shove as if someone were right behind me. As I staggered forward a few feet, I finally started seeing the real world again.

"What just happened?" I exclaimed, spinning around in surprise.

"It's okay, Leoman," said a ghostly black figure with a green hooded cloak and a silver "M" carved into it. "I'll help the DSI agents. You stop that maniac from poisoning the city."

"I'm already on that!" I exclaimed. "But who the heck are you?"

"I am Mirage," his voice quietly echoed as he quickly faded away into the shadows.

"That was really weird," I said quietly to myself.

CHAPTER 12

HOW DO YOU BREAK THE MIND-BREAKER?

I shook off the feeling and refocused myself on the task at hand: stopping Mind-Breaker. So I searched through the facility when I finally heard Annie's voice thank to my newly restored lion-like hearing. I found my way to the Plant's pipe room, running as fast as I could. By the time I got there, he was standing a few feet away from where Annie was strapped down onto a lab table. He was staring at the glowing acid green FANG formula coursing through the see-through hard plastic pipes, with his back to her.

"So what do think of this achievement, my beloved daughter?" he asked, calm and composed.

"You're poisoning the city, you maniac! And I'm not your daughter!"

"I know, I know. It's okay, sweetie. As soon as Daddy's done turning this city into his servants, he'll restore your memory."

"You're not my dad! How many times do I have to tell you, you creep?"

I'd had enough with Mind-Breaker and tried to take him by surprise.

"That's enough, Mind-Breaker!" I roared, lion-like, as I tried to pounce on him.

As soon as I came within inches of him, I was stopped by an invisible force that held me in midair as if I were paralyzed.

"So you're the lionhearted Leoman?" he asked confidently. "Or should I say, Mr. Leon Garrett?"

"It's Leoman to scumbags like you, Martin Baker," I said, straining and failing to break free of his telekinetic grip on me.

"What?" he exclaimed as he hurled me into a nearby wall with just a movement of his arms. "How do you know my real name?"

"Because it was you who murdered Big Daddy Jackson!" I said.

He started laughing at me as if I had told him a hysterical joke.

"I must say, you're not much of a detective if you just figured that out now!" he continued, laughing. "But now, if you'll be kind enough to leave my daughter and me in peace, maybe I'll let you live!"

"Not going to happen!" I roared as I pounced on him again to no avail.

"You young fool!" He chuckled. "Don't you understand? As long as I have my FANG formula coursing through my veins, I am a god!"

I realized I couldn't defeat him head-on, so I decided on another way.

"If you think you're so powerful, try to hit what you can't see!" I taunted him as I tore open a steam valve, which released a cloud of steam that prevented him from seeing me.

By the time his eyes readjusted, I had disappeared into the surrounding darkness.

"Where are you, Mr. Garrett?" he shouted. "Come on out so I can see you, you little brat!"

"What's the matter, Baker? Aren't gods supposed to be all-seeing and all-knowing?"

He ripped part of a large section of pipes with his telekinesis to find where I was hiding.

"Whoops, missed me!" I taunted him again.

"So, Mr. Garrett, how did you deduce my identity when the police couldn't?"

"Because I did some back-tracking on your history."

"What? What are you talking about?"

"I learned about what you said to Annie at the interview you had with her. But you were holding out on the truth with her, weren't you?"

"You're babbling, Mr. Garrett!" he shouted as he ripped another section of pipes.

"Am I, Mr. Brian Jackson? I mean, that's your real name, isn't it?"

"That's not my name!" he screamed.

"Oh, but it is. Brian Jackson, son of the late Benjamin Jackson and younger brother to the late Byron Big Daddy Jackson!"

"Shut up!" he screamed.

"Ooh, sounds like someone's got an inferiority complex!" I taunted him again. "Or was it just plain jealousy that you killed your dad and your brother?"

"I said shut up!" he screamed.

"But that's not all, was it? After the birth of your daughter, your late wife, Brianna Jackson, found out about the kind of man you are, and she hid her away from you!"

"No! No! That's not true!" he screamed.

"You killed her because she wouldn't tell you where your daughter was hidden!" I shouted as I finally appeared behind him on top of the control panel.

"You're lying!" he screamed as he hurled a section of pipe at me, which I evaded.

As I landed right in front of him and grabbed him by the neck.

"You think I'm the monster? Take a good look in the mirror while you're in No Man's Land for conspiracy and murder!"

He raised his hand to my face and started to break my mind with his telepathy.

"Well done, Mr. Garrett. Well done. You've discovered everything there is to know about me. Your healing abilities may give some defense against my power, but you'll end up the same way as everyone else who's been in my way—beaten and broken!"

As my head felt like it was about to explode, I found myself looking at Annie for I thought for the last time.

"Daddy!" She shouted. "Daddy, stop it!"

Mind-Breaker dropped his hand in surprise and shock, taking his focus off me.

"What did you say?" he asked, almost in tears.

"It's me, Daddy!" she said. "It's me, Maria!"

Tearfully, he released her from her straps and gave her a big hug.

"Oh, my beautiful daughter! I just knew you would remember me!"

"Of course I would! I'll always know who my father is."

And as he embraced her again, she took the opportunity to steal one of his syringes of FANG formula and inject it into herself.

"Maria! What are you doing?" he exclaimed in horror.

Her eyes glowed teal blue instead of the normally acidic green, and she realized she had gained the same telepathic and telekinetic powers he had, as her whole body started glowing all over!

"You're not my father!" she said. "You're just the man who murdered my mother!"

With a single punching motion, she sent him flying across the room, and he landed on the floor unconscious.

"Leon," she said, "are you all right?"

"Don't worry, Annie." I sighed as I staggered to my feet. "I'll be all right."

Just after we exchanged smiles to one another, we felt the ground shaking as if there was an earthquake!

"Leon, we have to get out of here!" she exclaimed.

We ran outside all the way to where Agent V was waiting for us.

"Agent V!" I called out.

"Leoman," he replied, "did you stop Mind-Breaker?"

"Yes, but the control panel was smashed during the fight," I replied. "Take Annie and get out of here!"

"What are you talking about, Leon?" she asked. "We've got to get out of here now!"

"Wrong, Annie!" I said. "You have to get out of here! I've got to stop that gas before it poisons the whole city!"

"How are you going to do that?" she asked.

"The FANG gas is being dispersed through the smokestacks," I said. "The only way to stop the gas is to pull them down!"

"Hold it, Leoman!" he said. "If you do that, you'll bring the whole chemical plant on top of you!"

"I'm sorry, Jamie," I said sadly, "but it's the only way to end this!"

I took off running toward the chemical plant, leapt up to the side of the building, and climbed my way to the top up of it where the two massive smokestacks towered above me, one to my left and one to my right. Using all the remaining strength I had left, I pulled them both together. With a huge *crash* of the two smokestacks colliding, it started raining large chunks of debris, which fell and piling on top of me.

To this day, I don't know how and I don't know why, but I managed to survive thanks to a slab of rebar being on top of me. Despite a lot of bruises and a few broken bones, I managed to lift the chunk of debris that was on top of me and staggered out of the rubble.

A couple of hours later, I was back in the hospital with Annie in the same examination room as Leon and saw her crying about me.

"Hey, Annie," I said, smiling.

"Leon?" she said as if I had just returned from the dead.

"I know I've got a lot of things to explain, but—" I said before I was interrupted by her kissing me.

"I love you, Leon," she said.

That's when my jaw flat-out dropped.

"You … you do?" I said, shocked.

"Yes," she said. "I've been meaning to tell you for a long time."

"But because of my secret, you couldn't tell me," I said.

"Yes, and I am so sorry!" she said, almost crying.

"That's okay, Annie," I reassured her. "I love you too."

We shared one last kiss before parting ways.

"Annie?" I asked. "Are you going to be at church next Sunday?"

"Yes, why?" she asked.

"Because I'm going to rededicate my life to Christ," I replied.

"That's great, Leon!" She smiled. "I'll be there."

"Great," I said. "Well, I guess I'll see you then."

"Okay. Well, good night, Leon," she said.

"Good night, Annie," I said.

She turned over in her hospital, and I turned over in mine in the opposite direction, finally falling asleep in the quiet, peaceful night.

Sunday came, and the pastor called me up to the front of the sanctuary.

"Leon Garrett has come before the church today to rededicate his life to Christ," he announced. "Leon, do you love the Lord with all your heart, all your soul, and all your mind?"

"Yes, sir. I do," I replied.

"Leon, do you believe that God sent His son, Jesus, to die on the cross for your sins?" he asked.

"Yes, sir. I do," I replied.

"And finally, Leon, do you promise to walk by faith and to follow in His ways?" he asked.

"Yes, sir. I do," I replied.

"Then, Leon Garrett I proclaim you as a son of the living God!" he said.

As the congregation filled with all my family and friends stood and applauded for me, I found myself wondering what God had in store for my life. Even though I'm still not certain to this day, I think I have a fairly good idea.

EPILOGUE: WHAT IS HAPPENING TO JOE?

A few days after I rededicated my life to God, Annie and I went to visit Joe in the hospital on an early evening. We were surprised to find he had made a complete recovery despite his near-death experience. It looked as if Agent V's special medical team managed to do a good job of saving my best friend after all.

"Can you believe it, Leon?" Joe said, smiling happily. "In a few hours, I'll finally be out of here!"

"All right!" I smiled back. "That's awesome, bud!"

"And looks like two somebodies are now a couple?" He chuckled as he noticed Annie and I holding hands.

"Hey, now," Annie said. "We're not married, you know!"

"Not yet, anyway." I chuckled under my breath.

Annie gave me a light shove, just as a joke.

"So," Joe asked quietly, "what do you think happened to Mind-Breaker?"

"Well, my dad said the police haven't found his body in the plant wreckage," I said, "so he may have survived and might still be out there making the FANG drug, along with the bounty on Leoman's head."

"Don't worry, Leon," Annie reassured me. "I know you'll get him."

"Are you sure about that, Annie?" I asked. "After all, he's still your biological father."

"No, Leon," she said sternly. "He is not my father."

"I'm sorry, Annie. I didn't mean to hurt your feelings."

"I know. It's okay. Don't worry." She sighed.

A nurse came into the room.

"Excuse me, you two," she said, "but it's time for Mr. Vantrice to get some rest, okay?"

"Yes, ma'am," Annie replied. "Time to go, Leon."

"All right," I said before turning to Joe. "Hey, get some rest, buddy."

"Oh, don't worry about me, Leon," Joe replied. "I will."

Annie and I were escorted out of Joe's hospital room.

"So, Leon, do you want to come over to my house and study?" Annie asked.

"Sure, but will your parents be okay with that?" I asked.

"I already asked them, and they are fine with it," she replied.

As we walked down the hallway holding hands, all the lights in the hospital started flickering around us. The lights went out as if it were a blackout. Instinctively, we looked at each other and ran all the way back to Joe's room. There, we saw the unbelievable sight of Joe floating above his hospital bed, with glowing green electrical bolts coming from the nearby electrical outlets and into himself. With a blinding flash of green light, the electricity stopped flowing into him. His whole body glowed with an unnatural green light.

"Joe …?" I asked calmly and cautiously. "You still with us, buddy?"

"What do you mean still with you?" he exclaimed. "I'm glowing in the dark!"

"Joe, it's okay," Annie said calmly. "Let us help you."

A hospital orderly came in, and when he saw Joe, the orderly tried to grab his radio. That was a big mistake, because as soon as he turned it on, it exploded in his hand from the sudden power surge.

"Oh, no!" Joe exclaimed. "I didn't mean to … oh, no! Oh, no, no, no, no, no, no!"

As Joe panicked and ran away. We tried to stop him, but he just ran through us as if we were not even there, like a ghost.

"Wait, stop Joe!" I called out.

"Come back, Joe!" Annie called out. "Please!"

"No, stay away from me!" he called back. "I don't want to hurt you guys!"

Something told me this was just the beginning.

As we tried to follow him, we realized he was moving too fast for us to catch up to him in the hospital hallway—at least too fast for a normal human to catch up to him.

"Leon, we need Leoman," Annie said quietly.

"I agree. Stay with him as much as you can. I'll catch up as soon as I can."

We parted ways, with Annie chasing after Joe while I went to a nearby bathroom with my backpack to change into my Leoman costume.

A few minutes after I finished, I ran to a nearby staircase and climbed all the way to the roof top without breaking a sweat. I used my animal-keen senses to track Annie by the scent of her perfume and began leaping from roof top to roof top to catch up to them while they ran off the hospital grounds. When I finally caught up with Annie, she was running after Joe while dodging the sparks and broken glass of Joe accidently shattering the lamp posts by uncontrollably sending electrical power surging through them.

"Joe, stop! We can help you!" I shouted after I landed in front of him from a nearby roof top onto the street to stop him from running.

"No way!" he exclaimed. "I might hurt you!"

"Trust me, Joe, there's not a lot of things that can hurt me that I can't heal from."

"Well, I'm not taking that risk, Leon!" he exclaimed. "Now, stay back before I fry you!"

"Joe," Annie said calmly, "listen to me. Just close your eyes and take a deep breath."

"Are you sure about this, Annie?" he asked.

"Yes, Joe," she said calmly. "Now, breathe in through your nose and out through your mouth."

"All right, Annie." He sighed. "I trust you guys."

He took a deep breath, and within moments, the green glow on his body faded away and the electrical discharges dissipated as he once more looked like his normal self.

"Yes! Wow, it worked! I'm human again!" he said calmly and happily.

The police arrived. They got out of their cars, drew their guns, and pointed them at Joe and me.

"Both of you get on the ground!" one of them shouted. "Hands on your heads now!"

At the sight of Joe starting to spark with green electricity again, I started trying to talk him out of getting too nervous.

"It's okay, Joe," I said calmly. "I'll take care of this. Just don't do anything rash, okay?"

"I'm trying, Leoman," he said slightly agitated. "Believe me, bud. I'm trying."

"Miss!" another one called out to Annie. "You need to step away from the vigilantes right now!"

"Not gonna happen!" she exclaimed. "Leoman has just recently saved this city from a chemical attack!"

"You need to step away, miss!" the officer shouted. "These two individuals are dangerous vigilantes with inhuman powers who are taking the law into their own hands!"

Despite their efforts, Annie remained by our side.

"Like I said, officer," she said sternly, "that's not gonna happen!"

As we stood in a standoff against the police officers, waiting anxiously for one of us or one of them to spark off an all-out fight between us, I found myself wondering if this was God's way of calling the three of us home to heaven above.

Just as I thought we were going to be filled with bullet holes, a bright spotlight flashed on from a hovering helicopter all of us, blinding us for a few seconds. I felt what seemed like half a dozen hands pinching at once in my left arm. When I looked down at my arm, tranquilizer darts were sticking out of it, and I started to feel weak and lightheaded again.

"No, not, not again," I groaned before collapsing to the ground.

Before I passed out, I saw Agent V of DSI walk up next to a police officer.

"It's all right now, officer," he reassured him. "We'll take it from here."

I passed out, not knowing what in the world DSI was going to do to us.